CW00404692

Green Ice

GREEN ICE

RAOUL WHITFIELD

NO EXIT PRESS

1988

No Exit Press
18 Coleswood Road
Harpenden, Herts AL5 1EQ

Copyright 1930 Raoul Whitfield

All rights reserved. No part of this book may be reproduced,
stored in a retrieval system, or transmitted in any form
or by any means, electronic, mechanical, photocopying,
recording, or otherwise, without the written permission
of the Publishers.

British Library Cataloguing in Publication Data

Whitfield, Raoul
    Green Ice – (No Exit Press vintage crime)
    I. Title
    813′.52 [F]   PS3545.H656
    ISBN 0 948353 13 9
    ISBN 0 948353 14 7 (pb)

9   8   7   6   5   4   3   2   1

Printed by Guernsey Press, C.I.

TO
Louis Este

CONTENTS

·1·

OUTSIDE

It wasn't the rain that bothered me. I'd felt rain striking against my face often enough, in the prison yard, during the last two years. It was being outside that worried. Sound that was different, traffic, so much movement. So many things going on at once. Confidence was something that a stretch in stir could nibble away at, destroy day by day and night by night. This wasn't routine, this freedom.

I leaned up against the wet brick of a two-story building, perhaps a dozen squares from the prison gate, let the rain drip off the brim of my new, soft hat—and stalled for time. A square to the northward traffic was heavy. Offices were closing up for the day; at intervals I caught the shrill sound of a traffic cop's whistle. I started northward, swore at myself a few times, stopped. It was no good acting this way. There was nothing to be gained in trying to beat something that couldn't be beaten this way.

I could get across down there, easily enough, and it wasn't the thought of the cop's uniform that stopped me from moving on. I didn't want to wet-nurse myself, that was all.

Trucks and machines were moving fast. It had been raining all day—and there was a lot of mud around. I moved away from the brick of the building and headed for the curb. A cab came around the corner—there was a squeal of brakes. The front wheels spurted water over the cuffs of my trousers—a door shot open.

"Mal!" The voice kicked my nerves around a little—I hadn't been expecting it. "Why didn't you wait? Didn't the warden—"

She was leaning out in the rain—and she looked like the devil. Too much art work around the eyes, and too many little lines around the lips. She went right on with a lot of talk, and after a while just got out of breath.

"Decent of you to come up, Dot," I said. "You look great."

The driver had a flat face out in the wet—he pulled it back under cover.

"Get in, Mal!" she urged. "I've got so much—to tell you—"

I shook my head. "Sorry—but you haven't got anything to tell *me*, Dot. It wasn't sensible—your coming up here. Grange said you were coming—I wanted to walk around. How'd you find me?"

She was staring at me with wide eyes. Rain was making little sounds as it hit her close-fitting, beige hat.

"There was a man in uniform—at the gate," she said. "He said you were walking around through the town, he guessed. He said a lot of—them do, after they come out."

I nodded. The flat-faced cab driver had his head out in the rain again; he had a half grin showing.

"Please get in, Mal!" she murmured. "It's been a long time—"

I smiled. But I hadn't the slightest intention of getting inside the cab with Dot Ellis. It *had* been a long time, but not for her. And why she had come up to the prison town from New York was something I couldn't figure—

not right away. It didn't interest me much. I'd got over a lot of things living behind the walls—Dot was just one of them.

"Nice of you to come up," I said foolishly, "but silly, too. That's all finished, Dot."

She looked sort of frightened. The driver jerked his head out of the rain. Dot started to whine, but I cut in.

"It's all right, Dot. It wasn't so bad—in there. I may call you up some time. Got to look around a little—"

"Mal!" Her head was out in the rain again, her dark eyes looked like those of a scolded kid. She wailed: "Mal—you wouldn't just let me go back without—"

"I would—just," I cut in cheerfully. "Pick up some fresh juniper juice on the way home—and mix as usual. You always could forget easily, Dot—and the gin'll help. I'll call you up—"

"Mal—"

I was sick of hearing that syllable already. The cab driver's flat face was out in the rain again. He was grinning. I started to shove the door shut, and Dot started to act up.

"You goddam highbrow!" she flared. "You always did think you were too good for me! You can't hand me *that* line, Mal Ourney! Jeez, Mal—"

I turned my back and walked away. Dot kept right on yelling. She was using up a lot of her old words, and she contradicted herself twice in every sentence. It sounded to me like a lot of after-the-gin raving. I got self-sympathetic.

"She's only the gal I did the two-spot for," I muttered. "She's been partying for my coming-out, and I turn her down cold. Poor little gal!"

The cab door slammed. Her final words were to the point, but they weren't true. Jane Ourney had been a lot of grief to Sam Ourney, but I *was* their honest-to-God brat.

When I turned around, the cab was a half block away.

I guessed that Dot Ellis was still raving. She'd lost most of her looks since I'd taken the rap for her little manslaughter act. Maybe she figured that was why I turned her down. She was all wrong there. When Dot drove the roadster up on the safety aisle, two years and a month or so ago, she was twenty minutes ahead of me. In just that length of time we'd have been out near Van Cortlandt Park. And I'd have told her that it was all off.

But I couldn't tell her while they were dragging the two bodies out from under the car—and while I was sliding back of the wheel and shoving her into the seat beside me. She'd have been sober by the time we reached the park, maybe. After the accident—she'd been hysterical. Trial by jury—two years in the Big House. She'd come up to meet me. She'd been late. I'd told her something that wouldn't have made much difference two years ago, and didn't make any now.

I was getting too wet for comfort. A cruising cab came along, and I got inside. I wouldn't cross the street, after all.

"Railroad station," I told the driver. "Don't hurry— I want to look around."

This one had a mustache and glasses. His cab was warm and clean. There were a lot of signs in it, most of them silly. He drove slowly, but that didn't seem to stop the skidding. He was an artist at it.

It was five-twenty when the cab pulled up in front of the railroad station. I got out and paid. Another cab pulled up. I looked at the flat-faced driver of it and swore. He was scowling as he twisted around and jerked open the door. I turned my back—and then the driver yelped.

"Jeez!"

He put a lot of feeling in the proper noun. I swung around, and he headed toward a figure standing out in the rain. A slicker-covered figure—a cop. I didn't want to look in the cab, but I looked.

Dot Ellis was slumped down in the seat—her head twisted to one side. She looked bad. One bullet had caught her in the throat, another had dug in about an inch above the bridge of her nose. I took a quick look around. There was nothing in her hands, and I didn't see a gun in the car. The flat-faced driver was yelling at the traffic cop.

I walked into the station, trying not to talk to myself. That was a Big House night habit. I grabbed a pill, lighted it. My fingers were steady enough. Dot Ellis was dead—murdered. Murdered a half hour or so after I'd been turned loose from doing a two-year stretch that had belonged to her.

There was some thinking to be done, and I wasn't in the humor for it. I could figure that the cab driver would tell the traffic cop what I looked like, and what Dot had called me. I couldn't figure much beyond that. A record was shooting words through a loudspeaker. I made out a few of them, but not enough. A porter passed me, and I asked him what it was all about.

"Local for New York—two minutes," he stated in a weary voice.

I wasted thirty seconds figuring what I'd better do—and a minute in buying the ticket. That left me thirty seconds to get aboard. When I dropped into a seat in the smoker a head pivoted around on a neck—the other end of the man's spine was on the seat ahead of mine.

"Hello, Ourney!" The man had a thin voice. "Got aboard, eh?"

I smiled. "Not quite," I stated. "The train was pulling out—so I went down by boat."

Steiner smiled, too. The train started to jerk. Steiner let his thin words just reach me.

"Yeah?" he said. "Better than going by taxi, eh?"

I closed my eyes a little, and decided that the fence who had been released from Sing Sing two days ago knew something. He had the face and voice of a girl, the courage of a rat—and the brains of a fence. I'd learned that over the two-year stretch.

"I don't like cabs," I stated lazily.

When I opened my eyes Steiner was still smiling. He looked more like a woman when he didn't.

"They're bad for frails," he said almost gently. "I remember one who went to sleep in a cab—and never woke up."

I looked out of the window. There was a lot of water on the glass—the train had come along from Albany.

"No?" I murmured. "You've been around. Heart disease, was it?"

Steiner chuckled. When he did that he stopped being like a woman.

"Lead poisoning." he explained. "Too bad, eh?"

I got up and headed for the coach up front. Steiner was still smiling.

"Terrible," I agreed. "It frightens me."

2

It didn't exactly frighten me, but it worried me. My grapevine line on Herb Steiner was pretty complete. He rated a minor part in the historical treatise I'd prepared—and which was never to go down on paper. Steiner was a minor crime-breeder. But I couldn't figure him in this. He was a killer. The law had never caught up with him. Maybe he was a better killer than he was a fence.

The big kick was that either he'd done for Dot Ellis, or he knew more about it than I did. Perhaps a bigger kick was that he had wised *me* up—in so-so fashion. The reason for that was too stiff. I went ahead a little, mentally.

Dot Ellis was dead, murdered. It was generally known that I'd stood her rap. It wouldn't take long for the quiet-clothes boys to put two and two together—and get five.

When the cab driver spilled the works about what Dot had called me, I'd be wanted for conversation. But I couldn't see much beyond that. I could find the driver who *wasn't* flat-faced—the one with the mustache and goggles. And that wouldn't leave more than a couple of minutes during which I was alone, after the flat-faced driver had taken Dot away.

That was the trouble—the boys would get five—when they needed four. My best bet was to slide off the train at the next stop—and go back up the river. Get it over with in a hurry.

Somehow, the more I thought about it the more I disliked the idea. It was sensible enough. It clicked along nicely. But there was Herb Steiner back in the smoker. Steiner knew more than I did—and *he* wasn't going back. I hadn't turned loose a small caliber gun on Dot Ellis. I hadn't seen her, until twenty minutes or so ago, for two years. And you never could tell about bulls or cab drivers. I talked to myself a little.

"Dot's out of it—Herb Steiner's in it. He's part of my show. How does he figure? Why does he figure? I'll stay along—and if they want me they'll find me."

I talked to myself at intervals until the train reached One Hundred and Twenty-Fifth Street, when I strolled back and watched Steiner drop to the platform. He didn't look around. I got off, too. There were some men waiting on the platform—but not for Steiner. Nor for me.

The fence bought a late addition of a tabloid, down on the street. He didn't read it—just glanced at the headlines, stuck it in his pocket. He hailed a cab, and even when he got inside he didn't look back.

I smiled grimly. There wasn't much use in tailing a crook who wanted to be tailed. There was a lot of sense in not tagging along. So I worked it that way. Inside a cigar store I called the number Donner had given me three months ago. First the line was busy, then there wasn't any such number—and then I got a wrong num-

ber. I went out of the booth and bought some pills. The
rain had stopped. I went back into the booth and tried
again. Right off the bat I got my number. I asked for
Joe Ross, and heard Donner saying that Ross was talking.
He used that name.

"This is Ourney," I told him. "Where do I come—
in about two hours, say? I want to pick up some clothes
and get a wash. It'll take that long."

Donner gave me an address and told me it was just
west of Sixth Avenue on Fifty-sixth Street. He asked me
what was new and I told him nothing was new. He said
he'd be waiting up—but that if I wanted rye I'd have to
bring it along. He had Scotch and gin. I told him Scotch
and gin would be all right, and hung up. I went out and
looked for a clothing store.

I felt a little tired, but already the fear of crowds and
traffic was beginning to leave me. I thought of Dot Ellis,
slumped down in the cab, up the river, and I thought of
Herb Steiner. I felt as though I needed to talk—and Wirt
Donner would be all right for that purpose. Just so long
as I talked the right way.

There was a gray suit I liked—and I went into the
store. The clerk was called to the phone while he was
hanging it on me. The connection was bad, and he kept
yelling the name of the gal to whom he was talking—it
was Dot. It began to get on my nerves, but finally he
hung up.

He was pretty sore when he reached my side again.

"Someday I'll murder that woman!" he muttered.

I told him the pants were too long, and he said that
was easy.

·2·

STOMACHACHE

I read a paper on my way down to Fifty-sixth Street.
Dot Ellis got more space than most of the other humans.
But there was one human that grabbed the headlines. His
name was Harry Cherulli—there was an "Angel" between the first and last names. He was a nightclub owner
and gambler, and he'd gone to the same place as Dot,
only about an hour later. That is, I guessed he'd gone
to the same place. I read the details on Dot first. After
all, two years were two years, even though I couldn't
feel heroic about serving it for her. She'd been drinking
my liquor before the accident.

The flat-faced cab driver had done most of the guessing. He'd had his hands full driving the cab. There was
more traffic than usual in the prison town. He'd had a
narrow escape from a smashup with a truck. He and the
truck driver had talked it out, and it seemed the flat-
faced driver was an ex-pug. Anyway, he'd climbed down
from the cab and had invited the truck driver to do the
same thing. The truck driver hadn't. Instead he'd almost
run the flat-faced one down. All this happened two squares
from the station. The flat-faced one guessed that this was

when Dot had been murdered. He hadn't looked back at her until he'd reached the station. He was too sore.

It sounded fishy. But a lot of things sound fishy that aren't. The bullets had been of twenty-two caliber—and in traffic they wouldn't make so much noise. The police were working on fingerprints in the interior of the cab, and they expected to make an arrest shortly. That sounded like the bunk. There was a brief sketch about Dot Ellis— there was nothing about me. I guessed that there hadn't been time. I'd come in for my share of publicity in the morning.

"Angel" Cherulli had been found in an alley behind his club, with a flock of thirty-eights in his stomach and chest. There wasn't a clue. He had many enemies. The rest of the story was just writing. I stuck the paper in my pocket and decided that there might be some connection between the two murders. I also decided that there might not be any. I remembered, however, that two years and a few months ago Cherulli had fallen pretty hard for Dot Ellis. It seemed sort of queer that they should both drop out of worldly affairs at about the same time. Cherulli I remembered as a short, thickset Italian with a cherub-like face. I'd played around his club, contributing some of the hundred grand a damn fool uncle had left to me because his only niece had married a Swede with big feet.

The cab was rolling around Columbus Circle. I stopped thinking about Dot Ellis and Cherulli. I was out of the Big House—my bankers had better than seventy-five thousand dollars in safe spots, and I had a job to do. Wirt Donner could help me—he knew some of the little crooks that had been squeezed. I was after the breeders of crime, and they weren't the little ones. There would be action; my mind and body needed it.

The cab stopped in front of the number Donner had given me. It looked something like a theatrical boardinghouse, only it wasn't in the right neighborhood. Or maybe things had moved uptown since I'd started to serve the stretch. I paid up, got out.

The door beyond the steps that led to the vestibule opened as I started to climb. Donner came out. He was bent over; he had both hands pressing against his stomach. Funny, thick noises came from between his lips. His head was twisted to one side.

"What's wrong?" I snapped, from a spot halfway up the stone steps.

Donner was swaying from side to side, hunched forward. His face was all twisted, and there was red on his lips. He tried to scream, but it was only a cough—a choking cough—when it came out.

Then he tumbled. I made a stab at grabbing him, changed my mind. His head hit the fifth step from the top, like a man diving into water. He went all the way down to the sidewalk. Across the street a woman screamed. I heard footfalls—someone running. It was a red-faced man; he reached Donner's side as I came down the steps. He bent over, straightened up right away.

"How do you figure in this?" he snapped at me.

I shook my head. "I don't," I said. "Saw the sign up there—went up to see about a room. He came out, holding his stomach, and tumbled."

The man with the red face nodded. He moved over close to me.

"I'm Donelly—Third Precinct," he stated. "This bird's dead—shot in the belly. Got a gun?"

I shook my head, lifted my hands a little. Donelly tapped around my new suit. I wasn't surprised to learn he was a dick—he looked like one.

A crowd was collecting. A cop came through. Donelly made his speech all over again.

"And stay with the dead guy," he ordered. "I'm going in the house."

I managed a faint smile. "Mind if I come along?" I asked. "I'll still take a room here, if you get the murderer."

The red-faced one didn't think that was so funny. He narrowed blue eyes on me. Then he looked up at the sign. It was one of those blue ones, with white letters. It read: "VACANCY." I'd seen it as I'd moved away from the cab.

"Come along," Donelly muttered, and started up the steps.

I went up behind him. Wirt Donner was dead—shot in the stomach. He had been a second-rate crook. Up in the Big House he'd always insisted that he'd been framed.

Donelly was shoving a bell. You could hear it ring— but nothing happened. He tried the door. It was closed, locked.

"Not so good—for you," Donelly muttered, giving me a quick glance. "He had a stomachache that killed him, but he stopped to close the door on the way out."

"Or someone shut it—after he came out," I added.

Donelly shoved the bell again. Nothing happened. Donelly swore. I looked down the steps. Another cop had come up. The crowd was growing. There were dirty curtains behind the glass in the door. A figure showed— the door was suddenly opened.

The woman had on a faded negligee. It was too long for her—it trailed dirty carpet. She had a pasty complexion, sharp features, and dopey eyes. She was around forty, maybe younger. Her blond hair was black close to the scalp. She looked sleepily at Donelly.

"You run this place?" he asked her.

She shook her head. "I stay here," she stated. "Thought someone left his key inside. Anything wrong?"

I figured she was lying, and so did Donelly. She wasn't so doped up or sleepy as she looked. The dick spoke.

"There's a dead man on the sidewalk. Come on down and see if you know him."

The woman smiled. She had nice teeth.

Quit kidding,'' she returned, and moved away from the door.

Donelly caught her by the arm. She started to act up. She screamed. Donelly swore and let her go. A fat woman came down the stairs. She started in by giving Donelly hell, and she ended by telling him that she was the landlady and that if he was a detective he was a great guy because her nephew was one, too. She went down the steps and looked at Donner's profile. She got kind of splotchy in the cheeks.

"My God!" she muttered. "It's Mr. Ross. He's— dead."

One of the cops said that he'd get the morgue wagon. The landlady said that Mr. Ross had lived in her house for three months; he had a hall bedroom on the second floor. He'd told her that he was a radio man, and he always had paid his bill a week in advance. He seemed quiet. That was all she knew about him.

Donelly said we'd go up to the parlor, if there was one. The landlady said there wasn't. We went up to the hall. The woman with the nice teeth had gone. Donelly told me to follow him, and we went up to Donner's room. It looked pretty neat. There was a quart of gin on a small table—a bottle of orange juice on the floor. The landlady looked surprised.

"I didn't know Mr. Ross drank," she stated.

"He's sworn off," Donelly returned grimly. "Ever see this gentleman before?"

He gestured toward me. The landlady shook her head.

"He looks something like my sister's first husband," she stated. "But I ain't never seen him before."

Donelly was poking around the tiny room.

"He was coming up to rent a place to sleep," he stated. "Funny, eh?"

I said that I didn't see anything funny about it. Donelly told the landlady to get everybody that was in the house downstairs in the hall—and asked her if she advertised her rooms to rent. She said she didn't except for the sign outside. She said it was a terrible thing—but that she didn't believe Mr. Ross had been killed in the house. She went out.

Donelly looked at me. "I was across the street when your cab stopped in front of this place," he stated. "You knew where you were coming. What's your name?"

"Malcolm Ourney," I stated. "You had a tip, eh?"

His lips twitched. He'd been across the street, and he'd seen the cab come up. Maybe that had been chance— maybe it hadn't. I figured it hadn't.

"Something like that," he stated.

"The murderer may be around the house," I suggested. "You're taking things pretty easy."

Donelly shook his head. "Not my precinct," he said. "Killer's gone away from here. Out the back way, I guess. Got a pal in back. Ourney, eh? How were all the boys up at Sing Song when you left?"

I just smiled. But I was thinking fast. Donelly was out of his precinct, and he knew something. He knew a lot.

"Pretty fair," I stated. "Jerry Coons died of pneumonia three days ago."

Donelly was poking around under the bed. He dragged out a suitcase.

"Yeah, I read about Jerry," he stated. "He always did have bad lungs. Got 'em doing night work around the Jersey City warehouses."

I was beginning to think Donelly was a bright boy. There was a lot of noise coming up from the hall below. Donelly stood up. He hadn't opened the suitcase. A deep voice reached us.

"Oh, Mike—I grabbed Salmon jumping fences!"

Donelly swore softly. He looked at me.

"Not bad, eh?" he muttered. "Red always swore he'd get Donner. Let's go down!"

2

He led the way. His name was Mike Donelly—he was a plainclothes bull. He knew that I was Mal Ourney, that Mr. Ross had been Wirt Donner, and that I had come along to see Wirt. He knew that I hadn't killed him, and he was pretty sure that one "Red" Salmon had done for Donner.

Red was pretty sick. He slumped on the dirty carpet of the lowest stair and talked a lot. He whined. He'd come over to see Donner, but he'd come in the back way because the police were riding him. He'd met Donner staggering down the stairs, and when he'd seen what was up he'd made a break for it. He hadn't heard any shots.

The second detective was lean and wiry. He produced a thirty-eight-caliber gun with a Maxim silencer attached. He stated that three bullets were missing, and that he'd taken the gun from Red.

"It's a dirty lie!" Red got pretty excited. "It ain't my rod—it ain't! It's a frame."

Salmon was undersized, pallid, redheaded. He looked like a sniffer. I stared at him while he whined. Donelly asked a few questions of everybody, and learned nothing. No one had heard even pop-coughs of a silenced rod. No one had heard Mr. Ross coming down the stairs. Donelly told his pal to take Red out. Red protested, and Donelly told him to shut up. He shut up. Donelly's pal took him away.

"That's that," Donelly said to me. "You still want to rent a room here?"

I shook my head. "No," I said. "And I don't think Red Salmon got Donner."

Donelly grunted. "You don't know so much as I do," he stated. "I haven't been boarding up the river for two years."

"Good enough," I replied. "Who gave you the tip that Red was after Wirt?"

The detective grinned. "If I told you that, you'd know as much as I do," he said cheerfully. "Red got Donner, all right. He'll burn for it."

I nodded. "He may burn for it," I agreed. "But he didn't get Donner."

Donelly swore softly. "Listen, Ourney," he said slowly, "I think you're a good guy. A lot of good guys go wrong in this man's town. Dot Ellis is out—and now Donner's out. You stood a rap for Ellis, and you didn't rate it. I spotted you right away. You don't know me, but I worked the Ellis case. She was a bum. Why don't you take a trip west?"

I grinned. "Why should I take a trip west?"

"Why should a guy live?" Donelly asked pointedly.

I didn't answer that one, but I got the idea. We moved toward the vestibule of the boardinghouse. We went down the steps together. The morgue wagon hadn't arrived yet. The lean detective and Red Salmon were standing near the curb. Two cops were keeping the crowd away. An elevated train clattered, a half block away. It had started to rain again.

Donelly smiled with his lips. "You got a raw deal with Dot Ellis, Ourney;" he said. "I looked you over before you went up. You're not a crook. Get out of town."

I nodded. "It might be a good idea," I said. "Who tipped you off to the fact that Wirt Donner was to get the works?"

Donelly's smile became a grin. "Santa Claus," he replied. "He's good that way."

I took a last look at Donner. He wasn't nice to look at. A siren wailed in the distance. I shrugged my shoulders.

"He didn't have anything to tell me, anyway," I said slowly.

Donelly swore. "He wasn't much of a crook," he stated. "Just one of the little guys."

"Just one," I agreed. "Maybe I'll take your advice, Donelly. Maybe I'll go away from the big town."

The detective with the red face grinned. He swore again.

"Maybe!" he muttered.

I walked eastward and reached Broadway. I needed a drink. Looking at an address on a slip of paper, I discovered that the flat of Ben Garren wasn't far distant. Crossing the circle I walked up along the park. It was almost eleven. The lights downtown give me a kick. At Sixty-seventh Street I turned westward, picked up the uneven number of the apartment house and went inside. It was a walk-up affair. I climbed two flights, going in as a woman came out, without ringing the bell. A radio was making a racket back of number thirty-five's door. I rang the bell.

Ben opened the door, stared at me, and cursed cheerfully.

"Damned if it isn't Mal!" he greeted. "Pull your hide inside. When did you get in?"

I walked inside and Ben closed the door. The place was sloppy with newspapers, and Cherulli's name was smeared all over them.

"I got *out* this afternoon," I corrected. "Dropped in for a drink."

Ben grinned. His face was dark with a stubble of beard; his small eyes looked tired. He ran his left-hand fingers through graying hair. The stone on his little finger glittered in the light from a cheap bridge lamp.

"Gin or Scotch?" he asked. "If you want rye—"

I groaned. "Gin," I said hurriedly. "You're talking the way a dead man talked—a couple of hours ago, when he wasn't dead."

Ben narrowed his eyes a little; they were shot with red and looked less colorless than usual. Ben didn't look so healthy as he had up the river.

"*Which* dead man?" he said slowly.

"Wirt Donner." I watched his brain send a little shiver through his body. "A runt named Red Salmon gave him a dose just now, over on Fifty-sixth Street. The quiet-clothes boys had a tip and grabbed Red. He's whining that he was framed."

Ben went over to a small table and squeezed a cigarette out of a half-empty package. He lighted up. He made a sucking noise through his nose as he inhaled. Then he walked out of the living room.

"I'll get the gin," he stated. "Want it straight or with juice?"

"Straight. Bring the bottle out. And some water." I sat down in a chair that felt soft, but wasn't. "I see by the papers that Cherulli got pumped out."

Ben Garren came in with two glasses, a bottle of gin, and some water in a silver pitcher. He went out and got another glass. He didn't seem to have heard what I'd said about Angel Cherulli. He poured me a drink. When he had his fixed I lifted the glass.

"Here's to Donner and Cherulli—and Dot Ellis!" I toasted. "I've got a hunch they're not so cold right now— as they look."

Ben Garren swore. "So Red got Donner, eh?" he muttered. We both drank. "He always said he would."

"Yeah." I leaned back a little in the chair. "That's what Mike Donelly told me."

The name caught him as he was swallowing the stuff. He choked around, said that he couldn't drink gin any-more, poured us both another drink, went over to the door and snapped a latch on the inside, came back and sat down.

I waited a little while and then asked a question. "Who got Cherulli, Ben?"

He laughed. It was a harsh laugh. He pointed toward the papers on the floor.

"Looks like a mob," he said in his rather thin voice. "Who got Dot Ellis, Mal?"

I lighted a pill. "I don't like bedtime stories, Ben," I returned. "Who got Wirt Donner?"

Ben made some more sucking noises. He looked hurt.

"Donner did Red some dirt on the witness stand, before he went up the river," he stated. "Red's been coking up—and talking too much. Red put Donner out, eh?"

I smiled. "Like hell he did," I said. "Are we going to just talk—or are we going to talk sense?"

Garren looked me in the eyes. He said: "You're rushing things, Mal. Why didn't you wait a few days? Why don't you put up with me and—"

"No, thanks," I cut in. "But I'll talk sense with you. Donner was small fry, Cherulli was getting big. I didn't know there was any connection between the two. And where does Dot Ellis come in?"

Ben leaned back in his chair and half closed his eyes.

"Cherulli wouldn't be good. He was taking graft without splitting—on the wet stuff. Dot Ellis was hanging around with him. She knew a lot of people he knew. She'd been drinking a lot lately. Maybe the mob figured she might yell around."

I nodded. "All right," I stated. "But what mob?"

Ben yawned. "Go easy, Mal," he advised. "I know what you want to do. It's a tough job. A lot of the small crooks won't like it. They'll be suspicious."

I smiled faintly. "Red Salmon would like it," I stated. "He's framed, and you know he's framed." Garren yawned and tossed off another drink. I tried the same thing, easing it down with a half glass of water.

"Maybe," Garren muttered. "But I ain't so sure. I've been pretty busy, trying to keep alive, and to keep away from some people."

I nodded. "You said you would, Ben," I reminded him. "It looks as though it's been a job. It looks as though I'll need help. I wanted Wirt Donner to help— he's out. I've got some coin—you're in, if you want the job. It's damned foolishness, but my stretch got me sort of attached to the idea. Playing in?"

Garren was frowning. "I'll tell you some things," he said. He lowered his voice a little, so that an orchestra from a dance club made more racket than his tongue. I got my chair a little closer.

"Dot Ellis knew you had some coin left," he said. "That's why she went up to see you. Don't get a swelled head and think she sat around and waited."

I swore. "Never figured that, Ben," I said. "She got drunk on my liquor—two years ago. That's why I shoved her out from behind the wheel, called a couple of witnesses liars, and stood her rap. She got drunk because I was going to tell her I was through. I wanted her to laugh it off—to tell me to go to hell. Was Cherulli hot for her just this afternoon?"

Ben shrugged. "You were up the river when she got the works," he stated. "Was it Cherulli's job?"

I groaned. "I haven't been outside for two years, Ben," I reminded him. "I wasn't in a mob the last time I was out. Don't ask me—tell me."

He shook his head. "Donner was a pretty good kid, Mal. And there might have been a chance for Dot Ellis. Talking straight—Red Salmon is a hophead, but he didn't do for Donner. Someone's sucking them in, using them. Someone always is, Mal. The big ones riding the little ones—using 'em. I've had it—since I got out. It's a fight—to even go half straight."

I took my third, and commenced to feel the other two. They loosened my tongue up a little, but they didn't deaden my brain any.

"I'm no damned philanthropist, Ben," I said. "But I've got about seventy-five grand I'd like to use in my own way. I don't like crooks much. You're not my idea of a great guy, Garren. Let's get it straight enough to make it count. You're weak. A lot of little crooks are weak. I don't like 'em—but I don't hate 'em. It's the big ones I hate—the breeders. The ones that suck in the little crooks—''

My voice was getting high and shaky. I got up, walked around, swore.

"Oh, hell!" I muttered. "You and Wirt Donner—you know how I feel. You knew up in the Big House. I haven't changed any. I've had a number. I've got a record. Manslaughter. You can learn a lot in two years, Ben.''

I sat down again. Ben Garren scratched his head noisily.

"I think there's a woman in it, Mal," he said slowly. "Up high, I mean. Doing it right, get that. A man, too. But some of the stuff has the touch of a moll.''

I nodded. "It takes two of a kind to breed something," I said slowly. "Crime's like a lot of other things.''

Ben Garren grunted. "You're talking too fast for me," he stated. "All I know is they got a lot of half-decent guys. They'll get more. What the hell do the bulls care? They make a show when they grab a hophead like Red.''

Some woman was singing a blues song. There wasn't much static, and you could hear the clatter of dishes in the nightclub. Ben turned his head toward the radio.

"Sounds like Babe Mullens," he said. "Cherulli was giving her a play. Big, nice-lined moll. Came out of Harlem to the glitter spots. Makes it and spends it. She can wail.''

I listened, and while I was doing that I saw Dot Ellis slumped in the cab. I got a flash of Wirt Donner pitching down the steps, hanging on to his stomach.

"What for?" I muttered. "They were in the way of something.''

Ben Garren looked at me almost sleepily. But he wasn't sleeping. I got up.

"You'll sit in with me," I said. I didn't ask it. "I'm

going to find a hotel, get some sleep. In the morning I'll
fix the loose change so that I can use it. I'll phone you—
and when we meet don't pack a rod."

Ben looked disgusted. "I never packed one in my
life," he stated. "What in hell good are they?"

"For some people—they're great," I said. "By the
way, know a woman that looks like this: pasty face,
sharp features, dopey eyes? She's around forty maybe
not that old. Blond hair, but it *was* black. Still black
close to her scalp. Lives in a boardinghouse over west
of Sixth, on Fifty-sixth?"

Ben shook his head. "I'm off women," he stated.
"And I don't like blonds. Why?"

I moved toward the door. "Figure it out," I evaded.
"I told you where she lived."

Garren yawned. "I've heard of that dick Donelly,"
he stated. "He's a bright boy they pulled across from
Brooklyn. He's an old-timer, at that."

I nodded. "He knew me," I said. "And I got the idea
the blond might have known Donner. You don't place
her?"

Ben shook his head. He came around and snapped the
latch on the inside.

"I don't figure we can do all our business in this
town," he said in a low voice. "Wherever we do it—
there'll be tough going."

"There'll be cigarette money," I returned. "A drink
now and then. It's tough going right now, isn't it?"

"You're damn right!" he stated. "Talk foolish over
the phone—I'll spot the good words. Some stoolie might
happen to be listening in."

He opened the door. I told him that I figured a small
store somewhere uptown would be the right place for
him, and I wished him luck. He told me to remember
him to the wife and kids. There was no one around to
hear us, but that didn't matter. I went down the stairs
whistling. On the last flight I stopped. A key was turning

in the lock of the entrance door. I started on down—the door opened a little. I whistled again. The door closed, and the woman turned around. She went out. I didn't get a look at her face.

She turned toward the park, and didn't look back when I was doing the same thing. I went toward Columbus, turned the corner southward. I stopped and lighted a cigarette. Then I got my face close to the corner of a store front and looked eastward on Sixty-seventh. I got a glimpse of the woman turning in toward the same flat house from which I'd scared her. She looked up and down the street for a second before she vanished from sight. Up toward the park there was a woman with a white dog.

I strolled back toward the odd number, went in, and tried the entrance door. It was locked. On the top floor, left, one H. Smitz lived. The card showed that. I pressed the bell. The lock didn't tick. The other top-floor card showed G. Blum. I tried that—and the lock ticked right away. I went in, but I didn't climb the stairs.

A door opened up above—after a while it slammed again. I waited about five minutes, then climbed three flights of stairs. The radio in Ben Garren's flat was still going, but it wasn't so loud now. Ben was talking. At intervals I caught words. He was swearing at someone. He was saying: "Jeez—cut it out, will you? Jeez—he was a bum! Jeez—what did you come up here for, anyway?"

A woman was sobbing. That was all she was doing, just sobbing. After a while the radio started to make a loud racket. I couldn't even hear the woman sob. It stopped suddenly—in the middle of a note. I took a chance and stuck close to the door. From somewhere beyond the living room I heard Ben yell. "Turn that thing on, damn you!"

And then I got the woman's words. She was talking to herself, flat-toned, monotonously. Her voice had a terrible sound. "He was—a good guy—he was—he never put me through—anything—he was a good guy—he was—"

Ben Garren cursed again, and I could hear him heading for the living room. I went down the stairs. The radio started when I reached the second flight. The blonde that Donelly had grabbed by the arm and invited to come down and look at Wirt Donner—she was up in Ben's flat. And he had told me that he didn't know a blonde— that he was off women. I knew that Ben was a liar.

I hailed a cab, named a small hotel not far from Broadway on Forty-sixth Street, and smoked two pills on the way down. Inside the room I stripped, lay on the bed, and talked to myself.

"Red didn't pump Donner out. Maybe the blonde did—maybe she didn't. If she did there was a reason. If she didn't—there was still a reason. She knows a lot about it. She had a yen for Donner. Ben Garren knows that. Maybe he knows more. I think yes. It's harder to figure Donner's go-out than the other two. Maybe they'll try to hang the Dot kill on me yet. Maybe not. Steiner counts. Cherulli isn't so hot in this—"

It went on for some time, and then I rang for the latest edition of three papers. Any three. I didn't feel the gin much, and I was pretty tired. All three papers agreed that Cherulli had been mobbed down, and that he rated it. Donner got a few sticks—a cheap crook done in by a hophead. One paper stated that Salmon had confessed and had collapsed. The other two stated that he was being grilled. Dot Ellis was played up as an example of a Broadway butterfly. The police up the river expected to make arrests shortly. That was in the earlier edition of the first paper I read. The other two had last-minute flashes. Dot had committed suicide. After a more thorough search a twenty-two had been found shoved down behind the cab seat. A police surgeon was quoted as saying that one bullet had only scraped the skin—the one in the throat had been fatal, but she had had time to stick the gun behind the seat. Time and physical ability.

I laughed that off. It meant that the police were going to give someone rope. Dot wasn't important, but they figured the killer was. The thing I couldn't get was why they figured they could bluff Dot's murderer into think- ing they believed she'd committed suicide.

I switched off the light beside the bed, tried to sleep. Two hours later I was still trying. And I needed sleep. A fat-faced bellhop came up, and I gave him a ten-dollar bill and told him what I wanted. When he brought it I let him keep the change and drank half the bottle's con- tents. It wasn't good Scotch, but it was good enough to put me to sleep. The last thing I remembered was that Donner had said he had Scotch at his place. And so had Ben Garren. But I'd had to buy it myself in order to *get* it. That seemed sort of funny, but I fell asleep while I was trying to figure why.

·3·

GOOD GUY

It was late morning when I woke up. I had a small headache, but as it was the first one I'd had in more than two
years it didn't count much. The papers came up with the
ham and eggs and coffee. The tabloids were playing Dot
big—and they'd got wise to a lot of things. My picture
was smeared around, next to Dot's. They'd found out I'd
been turned loose just before Dot had gone away from
earthly things, and the flat-faced cab driver had talked.
The chief of police of the river town was quoted as saying
that I'd be in custody soon. He had some questions to ask
me. My picture showed that I was tall, lean, and smooth-
shaven. It didn't show much else. Another tabloid had a
close-up. I looked almost handsome. It was a silly picture.
My lips were too full and my eyes too soulful.

I finished off the ham-and, drank the coffee, had a
shower, and dressed. Then I went down and got the prison-
town chief of police on the phone. His name was Baker.

"Malcolm Ourney calling," I said. "I see by the tabs
you're looking for me. I thought it might be true, even
if I did see it in the tabs."

Baker told me that it was true. He asked me to come

up the river. I said it had taken me two years to get *down*
the river, but if it was important I'd come up.

"It's important," he said. "Murder is always important."

I told him that maybe he was right, said I'd get up
there sometime in the afternoon. I asked him if I was
charged with murder, and he said I wasn't. Hanging up,
I bought cigarettes. Then I went downtown and saw Mr.
Hall, of Hall, Wickersham, Dunlop and Burns. Mr. Hall
acted embarrassed, said my uncle had been a fine man
and that he felt it must have been merely an accidental
and unfortunate circumstance that had involved me with
Dot Ellis. He got me some cash, arranged that some of
the money would be transferred to a convenient bank,
worked a lot of platitudes to death, and shook hands with
me. I went up to the Grand Central and waited for the
next train upriver.

While I was waiting, walking around, Donelly strolled
up to me. His face was as red as ever. He had his blue
eyes smiling, but it wasn't exactly a cheerful smile.

"Going away?" he asked.

I shook my head. "Going up the river to see Baker.
Want to come along?"

He shook his head. "What happened up there is out
of my line," he stated. "And what happened up at that
boardinghouse is all finished, and just too bad."

I nodded. "Just too bad that the sniffer's getting the
works for something he didn't start or finish," I said.

Donelly watched the faces of the crowd with casual
interest. He spoke almost carelessly.

"Salmon? We found him dead in his cell this morning.
Soft, at that. Pleasant dreams to the end, eh? Better than
getting the juice."

I let that sink in. Red was dead, and Donelly seemed
pleased.

"Sign a confession?" I asked, and kept my eyes away
from Donelly's.

"A real nice one. Fingerprints all over the rod, too. Well, nice trip, Ourney! I'm just up here to see the traveling salesmen come and go."

I nodded. "It's fun," I said without any particular expression. "Out of the Third Precinct a lot, aren't you?"

The quiet-clothes dick grinned. "It helps," he returned. "Hope they let you come on back, Ourney."

"Why?" I asked.

He moved off a little. "I'm all for reformers," he stated. "S'long!"

The gates were opened, so I went through and walked along the ramp. Red Salmon was dead. They had a confession. A lot of dope and maybe a little third degree. I forgot about that and started to think about myself. I needed information on Donelly—he knew things. That could wait. Ben Garren knew my idea; Wirt Donner had known it. Someone had talked. But just where did Donelly come in? I couldn't even come close to answering that.

Inside the smoker I grabbed a seat up front. There weren't many humans aboard.

"Cherulli's dead—and I don't give a damn," I muttered to myself. "Donner's out, and Red didn't do that. I didn't do it to Dot Ellis. I do give a damn about both of them. It's a dirty street all the way, but some of the debris is important—to me."

I got to thinking about what I could do with the money Dot hadn't gold-digged away from me. There were a lot of possibilities. But I decided that what I'd do with it would be a lot of fun. After that I dozed a bit.

2

Chief of Police Baker was a short, heavyset individual who talked very fast, squinted dark eyes over my head, smoked black cigars, and walked with a limp. His voice had a rasping quality. He started in by telling me that I didn't murder Dot Ellis, and that she didn't murder herself. I said that I knew one of his statements was right and that I guessed the other was right. He asked a lot of questions and I answered them all. He said that even if I didn't think much of Dot, he figured it was funny I hadn't climbed into the cab with her, after more than two years in the Big House. I got his point, but I just smiled. He said that he'd talked with Warden Collahan, and that it was his understanding that I was something of a noble soul. I laughed that off. There was a little silence, after which he squinted his eyes on my gray ones.

"Who killed Dorothy Ellis?" he asked.

I didn't laugh at that. I really believed that the chief wanted to know, and thought I knew. So I asked another question.

"I've been in prison for more than two years—how should I know?"

"That's how," he returned. "You've been in with a lot of potential killers for more than two years. A lot of 'em came out ahead of you—and a lot came in *after* you."

"I ran across damned few potential killers," I stated. "I lived a secluded life."

Baker smiled with his squinted eyes. He asked more questions.

"How about Herb Steiner?"

I expected that one. My answer was all set.

"He went outside ahead of me," I reminded. "I didn't know him very well inside."

Baker nodded. He kept right on smiling.

"There were fingerprints on the twenty-two," he said. "But they weren't Steiner's. Guess whose they were."

I swore. Not with any ill feeling, however.

"Mine?" I suggested.

Baker shook his head. I swore again.

"I don't like the game," I told him. "You tell me the answer."

"They were Dot Ellis's prints," he said. "It was her gun."

I sat back and thought that over. My first idea was that it might have been her gun, at that. My second was that it hadn't been her gun.

"I'm telling you these things because I'm aware of certain conditions," Baker said slowly. "The Ellis woman isn't so important—but she was running around with a mob."

I got the last statement, but I was more interested in the first.

"What conditions are you aware of, Chief?" I asked.

He smiled. "I talked with Warden Collahan about you. He knew something of your plans—he was quite sure you were not involved in the murder."

I nodded. Collahan had done precisely the thing I had suggested he would not do. He had been trying to protect me, and he had talked. I looked at Baker and tried not to show disgust. Baker smiled cheerfully.

"I'm not saying that I think your interest in cheap crooks is worthwhile, Ourney. They're weaklings. But if you can get to the big ones—help the police—"

I said slowly: "To hell with the police! I'm not interested in them—I'm interested in the breeders—the few who rope in the dumb ones, the weak ones—"

I checked myself. Baker looked hurt. I got up and forced a smile.

"Forget it," I advised. "I was drinking strong liquor last night—a celebration. I'm a little shaky. I'm sorry Warden Collahan talked to you about my plans, Chief. They may not go through—"

Baker's smile was hard. "That's right enough." There was an edge to his tone. "They may not."

I looked down at him. He got up. He spoke slowly, quietly.

"You didn't murder the Ellis woman, Ourney. Whoever did shot twice, under the cover of the traffic noise, when the cab driver was arguing with a truck driver. Then the killer shoved the gun in the fingers of her left-hand—got the prints, using cloth, of course. That was the mistake, Ourney. He got her left-hand prints, instead of the right. That queered the suicide gag."

I chuckled. "The hell it did," I stated. "Dot was left-handed."

Baker's lower lip dropped away from the upper. His eyes stopped squinting, widened. He sucked in a breath of air.

I grinned at him. He was swearing under his breath.

I said: "And still—it wasn't suicide, Baker. I knew that gal. She wouldn't have had the guts to go out that way. And why? Because she called me a flock of names and I didn't ride with her anyway? Not so good."

The prison town's chief of police was clicking his teeth together. He looked sore, and then he looked thoughtful.

"Left-handed!" he muttered. "You may be wrong, Ourney—she might have passed herself the dose, at that."

"She didn't. But whoever did—that human knew her well enough to know she was left-handed. And he gave you fellows credit for having more brains than you have. He thought you'd learn that fact, too."

"How in hell would we know?" Baker snapped. "She isn't local."

I lighted a pill. "She's local, all right," I stated. "She wasn't—but she is. If you don't want me anymore—I'd like to look at her. Rather, I wouldn't like to, but maybe I'd better."

"She's at the morgue," Baker said. "Tell me where I can get you if I want you."

I told him I'd give him a name and a box number after

I got back to New York. I told him I didn't think I'd go through with my plans—the ones I'd spoken to Warden Collahan about. I said I wasn't a crook, and I was getting sick of being close to them. By the time I got through I had put on a good show for him and almost believed what I was saying myself.

I went over to the morgue and looked at Dot. She didn't look so bad. There wasn't anything I could learn, but I felt better after I'd seen her. A morgue official told me her sister was expected from Rochester. I went down to a florist's and ordered up two dozen roses, white. The florist was tall and severe-looking; he got a jolt when I said they were for Dot Ellis, over at the morgue. He asked about a card, and I told him they were just from one virgin to another—so a card wasn't necessary. He didn't like that. I asked him about a speakeasy, and he brightened up.

He stalled around a few minutes and then took me in back. The whisky wasn't so good, but it helped. I bought him a drink and after a while bought him another. Then I asked him if he knew a flat-faced cab driver in town. He said that might be "Bun" Leary, that Leary had been a prizefighter and that he had driven the cab in which Dot Ellis had been murdered. He said that Leary was a good guy, only a little rough. But he didn't mix up with women. Then he tightened up and stopped talking.

"Maybe you're a detective," he guessed.

I told him that I hadn't got that low, that I'd known Miss Ellis some years ago, and that it was just too bad. He agreed, and I went down and found that the next train was due in two hours, but that I could get a bus in something like thirty minutes. Outside the railroad station I waited fifteen minutes and then picked up Leary. His face was as flat as ever.

He glared at me as I went over to his cab. I just grinned.

"Listen—" I said—"you didn't do for Dot Ellis. And

I didn't. You're a tough guy, and when you were scrapping you didn't have much of a guard. But they didn't hit your eyes so hard. I've got a twenty-dollar bill in my pocket that I don't care about keeping there. I'm going to show you something, and I'm going to ask you something. All I want is the truth. Will I get it—or won't I?''

It was a long speech, but he understood most of it.

"Maybe you're crazy,'' he stated. "But I ain't got nothin' to worry about. Give me the twenty first—show me, and ask. I'll answer you straight.''

"Fair enough,'' I said, and reached for the twenty-dollar bill.

3

It was dark when I got back to the city. It was colder. I went in somewhere and bought a fall overcoat—one that was short enough for leg movement without contact with the material. I looked up the name of Garren in the phone book and was a little surprised to find it. I'd figured it might be necessary for me to go down to his place.

He was in, and I talked nonsense, along with a few words that meant something.

"I've been up the line to look at that store location, and I've learned something you'll be interested in. Supposing I come up around nine?''

"It'll be all right, DeGroot,'' he replied. "And if you can get your hands on some cash, I could use it.''

"Sure,'' I said, "almost anyone can do that, if they can get their hands on it.''

I had some oysters that tasted like a million, washed them down with something that passed for beer, tackled a steak that was supposed to be medium-well and wasn't, drank two cups of black coffee, called the Third Precinct—and went to a movie. I had two hours to kill, and I picked a bad way to do it. After about a half hour I got out and walked down to the boardinghouse in which Donner had taken the dose. The fat landlady answered my ring, but she only opened the door a few inches.

She recognized me right away. I told her that I was looking for the woman who had let us in the night of the murder, last night. She looked blank—as though she'd never heard of any murder. I described the woman in the faded negligee. The landlady nodded.

"Oh, Ella," she said. "She went to Pittsburgh this mornin'. Went to visit her aunt. She was upset, she was. I don't know where her aunt lives. Ella Bock—that's her name. She's a good girl, Ella is. Maybe I can find you the address. It ain't just right, but maybe—"

She let her voice trail off. I assured her that everything would be all right. She was lying, and I knew it. She came back with a piece of paper on which something had been scrawled. She read it off.

"Six hundred and four, Third Street, South Side, Pittsburgh. Her aunt's name is Emily Munn. I guess it's—all right. It seems funny, but you're the police, ain't you? You was just bluffin' about that room, wasn't you?"

I nodded brightly, got out the stub of a pencil, and scrawled the address. I thanked her, went down the steps. A half block away I threw the slip of paper on which I'd scrawled the number into the gutter. I remembered the names. Ella Bock. Emily Munn. They might mean something. The address didn't. I wasn't so sure about Pittsburgh. The landlady had used the name of that city pretty quickly.

At Broadway I got the time from a store window. It was twenty minutes of nine. I called the Third Precinct again and was told that Donelly had left the station ten minutes ago. After that I hailed a taxi and gave the driver an odd number on Sixty-seventh Street, east of Columbus Avenue.

Ben Garren let me in and smiled cheerfully. There

was a bottle of Scotch in the living room, ginger ale and ice. We downed the drinks. Ben snapped the latch on the inside of the door.

"What's new?" he asked.

I sat down and took a pill, tossing the pack on the table.

"I've been up the river," I said. "Had a talk with Baker, the Big House town chief of police. He's a good guy, but dumb."

Garren grinned. "Most good guys are dumb," he said.

I let that pass.. "He's lined up the gent that did Dot in," I told Garren. "Got the goods on him right."

Ben widened his bloodshot eyes. He ran left-hand fingers through his hair nervously. He smiled.

"Yeah?" he muttered. "Who did the work, Mal?"

I looked serious. "Herb Steiner," I said slowly. "Figured it that way, myself."

"Hell!" Ben put a lot of feeling in the word. "Steiner, eh? Can you beat that! I'll be—damned!"

I shook my head. "Steiner was working for Cherulli, Ben. Someone spread the word that when I got out I was coming gunning for him. Because he was playing around with Dot, see? So Cherulli told Steiner to get Dot—and frame me. He came damn near doing it."

Ben Garren half closed his bloodshot eyes. He whistled softly.

"Can you beat that!" he muttered. "How'd he slip up?"

I grinned. "I had a perfect alibi," I stated. "I didn't ride with her, Ben. And Herb stuck around the town too long after he was turned loose. And then again—he forgot something. Something important."

Ben lighted one of my pills and waited for me to tell him what Herb Steiner forgot. I didn't tell him because I couldn't think of anything. Instead I leaned back in the chair and pulled on my cigarette.

"Ben—" I said slowly—"someone up in the Big House talked about what I was thinking of doing—when I got out."

Garren swore again. "It looks that way," he stated. "Donner, eh?"

I frowned. I took a sip of the Scotch and ginger ale and made a face.

"Can't down this stuff," I stated. "How about some water—and I'll take it straight."

Garren headed for the kitchen. "Sure thing," he stated.

I went over to the door and made no sound snapping the latch off. Then I went back and sat down. Garren came in with the water. He was grinning. He'd shaved, but there wasn't much pink in his face. He fooled with his hair, and the diamond glittered in the light again.

He sat down with his back to the door, shook his head slowly.

"Herb Steiner!" he muttered. "I didn't figure it that way."

I looked at the Scotch, but I didn't drink any of it. I half closed my eyes.

"Went over to the boardinghouse where Donner crashed," I said slowly. "I was looking for a sloppy blonde. Found out she just left for Pittsburgh this morning."

Garren's hands were at his sides—they came up convulsively. The muscles of his mouth twitched. Then he yawned. It was a poor job.

"What for did you want to see one of those dames?" he asked almost sleepily.

I grinned. "Wanted to ask her what she was doing up *here* last night," I replied.

He took it pretty well—all things considered. He stared at me, sucked cigarette smoke down into his lungs—let it come out slowly. He laughed hoarsely.

"That's not so bad," he said in a thin tone. "Now I'll tell the one about—"

"Don't." I let the one word come out sharply. "Don't tell any story even half so funny."

"I couldn't," he came back. "What in hell made you think any dame from a boardinghouse came up here last night?"

"My eyes. I saw her come up."

I lighted one pill from the stub of the other. My hands were at my sides—I was slumping comfortably in the chair. Garren blinked at me. Then he grinned.

"Aw, cut it out, Mal!" he muttered. "You've been drinking."

"Sure," I agreed. "With a florist up the river. And with a flat-faced cab driver named Leary."

Ben Garren got up from the chair. He went over and turned on the radio. It was a power set, and it just hummed. It had to warm up before it racketed.

"Ben—" I said slowly—"you're a rotten liar. You had a blonde up here last night. She was the one that Donelly grabbed, over at the address where Wirt Donner was put out. She was sort of hysterical up here, and you were damned sore at her. Why don't you come clean?"

He stood in front of me. He got a sheepish smile on his face.

"Mal—" he said—"I just didn't want you to think that dame had sucked me in. She's been playing me— and I've been playing her. She doesn't know what it's all about. I gave her my last coin and told her to break for the dirty burg. She just happened to be there."

I nodded. "Sure," I said. "And you just happened to be up the river yesterday afternoon."

"I don't get you, Mal," he said hoarsely.

"I'll make it clear. Very clear, Ben. You were wise to the fact that when I got out of prison I was going to shove in on some big-time crime breeders. Donner figured you were white—and he made a mistake. I figured the same way—and I made a mistake. When you lied to me last night I knew I'd made the mistake. But I hadn't gone all the way with you, Ben. You thought I was starting at the Donner kill end. I wasn't. You got a dame that knows something out of town—maybe to Pittsburgh, maybe not. That'll show up later. But you got her out of the way because you figured I was working the Donner kill.''

"Jeez—you're drunk!" Garren's voice was hoarse.

I shook my head. "I'm outside, Ben," I said slowly. "And you're not. You're inside, Ben. You're not a cheap crook anymore. You're a killer."

He was breathing hard. His eyes were on mine. I kept smiling.

"You might have been a big guy someday, Ben," I said. "You might have sucked in the little crooks, used 'em—let 'em take the raps. Let 'em burn. They never seem to get wise to the fact that the coppers aren't as dangerous as the big guys on the inside, on their side. But you won't be a big guy, Ben."

'You're nuts!" Garren's voice was a whisper now—a hoarse whisper.

"You're dumb," I told him grimly. "You let the flat-faced cab driver look at your face while you were trailing Dot. You stuck close to her. You watched other guys—but you got careless about Leary. You figured they'd grab me, Ben. You figured I'd be a sucker. You knew Dot was left-handed, and you gave her a small-caliber dose at close range, while the cab driver was gabbing with your pal, the driver of a light truck. You slipped off the back end—and gave Dot the works. Your pal did a lot of yelling—and two engines were running. You stuck the gun in her left-hand—then shoved it back of the seat. You—"

I stopped. Garren's right-hand was sliding up past his belt, toward his left shoulder.

"Donelly!" I yelled.

The door crackled under a blow. Garren whirled. I got

up and slugged him just under the right ear. He went to his knees as Donelly came in.

"You—stoolie!" he screamed.

His rod came up—Donelly's gun crashed. Once—then once again.

Garren let his right-hand drop. He raised his left a little. He sat down. He started to cry. It was pretty bad. Then he rolled over on his face. Donelly's face wasn't so red. He pulled Garren over on his back.

I took a picture out of my pocket. Ben's eyes were on it as I held it down so that he could see. It was a photo of Ben, with a straw hat shoved back on his forehead. Donner had given it to me, up at the Big House.

"I showed it to Leary," I said slowly. "And he said you'd been tagging Dot. You murdered her, Garren— and you tried to double-cross me. You—"

I stopped. Garren was trying to say something. There was a lot of racket outside the flat—people were running around. Donelly and I bent over Ben.

"The big—guys—wrote her—out." Garren was slipping off, going deep for air. "I couldn't—get clear— they had me—both ways—"

He quit talking. His body shook and then stopped shaking. Donelly fingered his right wrist.

"All done," he muttered thickly. "Christ—I don't like that."

I stood up, shut the door of the flat, snapped the latch, shut off the radio. I went over and opened a window. After a few seconds I came back and looked at Donelly. His face was getting red again.

"He had a rod out," he muttered. "I had to—let go."

I nodded. "That was your play," I said.

"Christ," Donelly breathed. "We figured he was going—straight."

I was staring at the back of the picture Donner had given me, up the river. Donelly looked over my shoulder

at the words Wirt had scrawled. He read them slowly.
" 'Ben's a good guy, Mal—look him up when you get
outside.' "

I looked down at Ben Garren. Donelly said in a grim
voice. "Well—you looked him up, Ourney."

I went over and poured two drinks. We didn't use
chasers. Donelly nibbled on a mint. After a little while
he went to the phone and called a number. I stood near
the window. Two things were certain. Ben Garren had
done for Dot, in the cab. There had been orders for the
job.

Donelly's voice reached me. Between words his teeth
crackled the peppermint he was chewing.

"Yeah, sure—that's right. Yeah, dead as hell. Sure—
I'll be waitin' outside."

· 4 ·

S T E I N E R

The third night outside went better. My nerves were less jerky. But the hotel rooms were small, and even with the windows opened the walls kept closing in. There was a radio playing somewhere, and I kept thinking about the one Ben Garren had been playing before Donelly's lead shoved him out of the land of dials and loudspeakers forever. I got some sleep, at that. The telephone bell woke me at ten minutes after eight; Donelly choked for a while, then got his words straightened out.

"Lentz wants to see you, down at Headquarters," he stated. "About the party last night—and maybe some other things. You'll be all right, Ourney."

I told him I hadn't much doubt about that, and that I'd show at Headquarters. It took me a half hour to get dressed, not rushing things, and with a shower thrown in for good luck. I didn't get so much kick out of brushing my teeth as I had in stir. After breakfast I cabbed down to Headquarters and met Donelly outside of Lentz's office.

"How'd you doze?" I asked.

He used up a few cuss words first, and then said that

he hadn't slept much. He said he never slept well after killing a guy, and his eyes looked bloodshot.

"You'd have slept better if Ben had used his rod first," I said. "More permanently."

Donelly nodded and didn't say anything. We went into Lentz's office and a fuzzy-haired girl asked us to wait a little while in an anteroom. She had a neat trick of chewing gum and humming at the same time. We waited ten minutes before she got the buzz. Donelly acted nervous. I got the idea that maybe he'd never met Lentz before.

We went in and Lentz gestured toward a couple of chairs. He was a man of about fifty with gray hair and a good chin. He looked more like a small-town merchant than the head of the New York detective bureau. His eyes were blue and wide.

"I'll save time and make a speech," he said in a rather thin voice. He picked up a sheet of paper from the surface of his desk and read in a monotone. "Thirteenth—Herb Steiner out of Sing Sing. Fence. Sixteenth—Malcolm Ourney out of Sing Sing. Two years—manslaughter. Ourney generally believed to have taken sentence for Dot Ellis, who drove car through safety aisle, killing two. Sixteenth—'Angel' Cherulli gunned out in alley back of his club—nightclub owner and big-shot gambler. Sixteenth—Dot Ellis murdered in cab at Ossining. Sixteenth—Wirt Donner, under name of Ross, shot to death in West Fifty-sixth Street boardinghouse. Served recent sentence in Sing Sing. Seventeenth—Detective Donelly shot Ben Garren, not long out of Sing Sing, to death in flat on West Sixty-seventh Street. Note—Malcolm Ourney was in Ossining at time of Ellis woman's death. Ourney was on the scene when Donner was murdered. Ourney was present when Detective Donelly shot Ben Garren in self-defense."

Lentz set the paper down on his desk, widened his blue eyes on my gray ones.

"For a man just out of the Big House—you get around," he observed in his thin voice.

I smiled a little. "It doesn't mean anything," I told him. "Some luck—and some headwork."

He nodded. "Separate the two—and tell me about the headwork," he instructed.

I thought that over. Donelly sat stiffly in his chair and kept his eyes on Lentz. The quiet-clothes boss didn't seem to know Donelly was in the room.

"Ben Garren murdered Dot Ellis," I stated. "He lied to me—and I tripped him up. He carried a gun, and I don't—so I had Donelly along. Headwork, maybe—maybe not. The rest was luck."

Lentz tipped his chair back and nodded.

"Sure," he agreed. "You were just outside, Ourney—beginner's luck, eh? You just happened to be in on Donner's murder—and you just happened to be the last one who chatted with Dot Ellis, up the river."

I shook my head. "I didn't chat with Dot. She bawled hell out of me. As for Dot—Donelly listened in on Garren's confession. The big guys had him both ways. He rubbed her out."

Lentz nodded again, smiling with narrow lips. He had a trick of rubbing his right eyebrow with right-hand fingers.

"What big guys?" he asked.

I just looked at him. "As for Donner," I said slowly, "I was just looking for a room—"

Lentz yawned. "All right, all right!" he interrupted. "Look here, Ourney. You're not a crook. Why don't you take a trip?"

"Where?" I asked.

He shrugged. "Paris is nice in the spring," he said. "And you are not a poor man."

I looked toward the windows. "I'm not a crook, you say. Then why run me out of the city?"

Lentz seemed hurt. He tilted his chair forward.

"A lot of things happen," he said vaguely. "You're not a crook *yet,* Ourney."

I didn't like that much. While I was thinking of the right answer Lentz said something that meant something.

"You're not a crook, Ourney—but you looked up a couple, just as soon as you got out."

I nodded. "One was a murderer," I reminded him. "That's why I looked him up."

Lentz smiled. "Sure," he agreed. "Here's another speech. You've gone reformer. You want to protect the little crooks from the big ones. So you start in by dragging in one of my men to shoot down a little crook. Does that make sense?"

I nodded. "Damn good sense," I replied. "I wanted Donelly to make the pinch. He's a good dick—and can stand promotion."

Donelly swore. "Thanks," he muttered grimly.

Lentz yawned again. "I hate reformers' guts," he stated in a thin tone. "We can handle the big guys our way."

I let that pass. "Dot Ellis was murdered. I did two years for her, Lentz. I owed her that. She came up to give me a coming-out party—and she was rubbed out. I wanted to know why—and I figured Ben Garren might tell me. He didn't take it that way. I'm no reformer."

Lentz looked bored. "Why was she put out?" he asked.

I tried to look just as bored, but it wasn't a success.

"Why was Wirt Donner put out?" I asked.

There was surprise in Lentz's blue eyes. He smiled.

"Red Salmon had a grudge. He did the trick—and confessed."

I laughed that off. "One of those things," I said. "Sure he confessed."

Lentz was getting annoyed. He cut out the suave stuff and said impatiently: "You're not the first human to do a stretch up the river, Ourney. And you're not the first one to come out with the idea that the police are all wrong and the crooks are all right. Did you meet up with any one of 'em who wasn't inside because he'd been framed?''

"Supposing," I said slowly, "you tell me just why you sent for me, Lentz?''

He stopped rubbing his eyebrow, leaned back farther in the chair, and smiled.

"I haven't got anything on you, Ourney," he stated. "Garren did for the Ellis woman. Red coked up and got a guy he hated—Wirt Donner. Cherulli had it coming and was mobbed out. Donelly here had to let go at Garren. That's a lot of killing—but it's all right. None of it was important.''

He stopped. Donelly looked more cheerful. I nodded.

"You got me down here to tell me none of it was important," I suggested. "All right.''

I got up from my chair. Lentz was smiling a sort of hard smile. His blue eyes were as wide as ever.

"But don't be so many places when things happen," he suggested. "Let the police take care of the bad boys, Ourney.''

I nodded again. "In other words, you figure I had an in on these murders—and you're telling me not to have any more ins.''

Lentz looked at Donelly and spoke to me. "Something like that, yeah.''

Donelly got to his feet. Lentz spoke in a quiet tone. "I'll see what I can do for you, Donelly. Never mind Cherulli—just routine.''

I moved toward the door—Lentz pressed a button and the gum-chewer came in. She smiled toward me, then toward another door. She spoke to Lentz. "Herb Steiner.''

Lentz smiled. "Hold him a few minutes, Nellie.''

I was near the other door. "Just a few cheap murders, eh, Lentz?'' I asked.

He kept right on smiling. "Something like that," he agreed. "They come in batches—but they don't mean anything. But the tabs sort of like 'em. I hope we understand each other, Ourney."

"I'm sure we do," I returned. "Give my regards to Steiner, will you?"

Lentz looked surprised. He raised his eyebrows.

"Steiner—didn't know you knew him, Ourney."

I got a hand on the knob of the door. Donelly was close to me.

"Oh, yes," I said. "We were inside together. You've got his name on your report, remember?"

Lentz acted as though he were just seeing the light. "Sure—sure. That's right. I'll tell him you were in to see me, Ourney."

"Thanks," I replied, and went out.

Donelly was right behind me. His face wasn't quite so red as usual. He muttered to himself, but I didn't get what he muttered. We went down the corridor together.

"A lot of fuss over three cheap murders," I suggested. "Maybe one of 'em counted."

Donelly stared at me. "Which one?" he asked.

I passed him a pill—lighted two of them.

"Donelly," I said slowly, "if you were half as dumb as you acted you'd still be a pretty good dick."

He kept on looking stupid. We went down to the street. Donelly took me by the right arm and got confidential.

"You don't think Red Salmon gave Donner that dose," he said. "Well, I'll tell you something. We got a tip that Red was going to do that little job—that's why I was there."

I groaned. "I believe you, Donelly—I believe you," I told him. "You got a tip—and a guy was murdered and Red was there, sure enough. And that means that Red did the job." ·

Donelly swore softly. "What's eating you?" he muttered. "We got a confession, didn't we?"

I laughed out loud. "Donelly," I said, "you can't get me worked up over the Donner kill. That isn't the one that counts."

The dick looked puzzled, but I had a strong feeling that he wasn't.

"What's eating you?" he repeated. "You did a two-spot for a dame that wasn't worth it. Now you come out and get all excited because a flock of little guys are bumped off."

"I'm curious," I told him. "But just the same—I'm running out on you. Going up to Boston to see my grandfather."

Donelly's face got redder. He started to get sore, changed his mind.

"Must be old as hell," he stated.

"A hundred and ten," I came back. "Want to come along and help me comb out his whiskers?"

The red-faced dick grunted. "After all," he said slowly, "Dot *was* your woman!"

That gave me a little jolt. Donelly was either clever or stabbing around in the dark. One thing was almost as bad as the other.

"Don't go to the trouble of going in one door somewhere and coming out another," he said quietly. "I'm not tagging along."

I grinned at him. "Thanks," I said. "If I run into anything good I'll give you a ring."

He dropped his cigarette butt and stepped on it. He swore.

"If you run into something *too* good, maybe the morgue'll give me the ring," he said grimly.

He went on his way without looking in my direction.

2

When I got back to the hotel the clerk gave me a little slip of paper. A call had come through. It had come from

a gentleman by the name of Herb, and he had requested
that I stick around until he arrived. I gave the clerk a
cigar and handed him back the slip of paper.

"Stick it in the box—with this—" I gave him the key.
"When Herb comes along let him see you looking for
it—and tell him I went out and haven't come back yet."

The clerk nodded. "How are you going to get in the
room?" he asked. "I've got the key."

I nodded. "The door isn't locked," I told him and
went on up.

Upstairs I thought of something else. I called the clerk
and told him to give me a ring when Herb arrived, but
to keep it quiet. I said that he'd probably go out right
away, after he was told I wasn't in. Then I packed a few
things in a bag—and smoked a few. The phone bell rang,
and the clerk told me that Herb had come in, had acted
disappointed—and had gone out.

I opened both windows and the door—let the cigarette
smoke clear up. Then I shut the door, locked it with the
snap on the inside. After that I went around behind the
door and lay on the floor. Five minutes passed—the snap
lock clicked a couple of times—the door opened a half
inch. Then another half inch.

Then it swung open—and I was behind it. Someone
came in and grabbed some sheets off the bed, took them
out near the doorway, and dumped them in the corridor.
Someone came back in and took off a coat and vest,
tossing them over the foot of the bed. I got a glimpse of
Herb Steiner. He whistled as he snapped open my bag
and went to work.

It wasn't a bad gag. With the sheets outside anyone
passing would think that the maid was inside—even if
they knew I wasn't. Herb figured I wasn't, of course.
And if a chambermaid came in she'd probably figure
Herb was the new guest. He had his coat and vest off.

He kept on whistling—and his whistle was as thin as

his voice. He was doing a good job with the bag. I stood up.

"Maybe the stuff isn't there," I suggested.

He straightened, his girl face twisted until it almost looked like a man's. He shrilled out something that sounded like "Christ!" His right-hand dropped.

I shoved the door out of the way—and hit him just as he was tugging at the rod. We both went down, only he was underneath. I gave him a knee in the stomach and a left that was meant for the jaw and landed over the right eye. The knee did the trick.

He groaned, rolled over on his side—flopped on his back. I took the rod away, went over and closed the door. I snapped the lock again. Then I went back and sat on the edge of the bed. Steiner was getting a little air now and then, but it came hard. His face was pretty white.

"A little crude, Steiner," I said cheerfully. "Though the lock work was not bad."

There was fear in his eyes—a lot of it. He was breathing heavily—and he touched the spot over his right eye with care.

He got up slowly—staggered around a little. He spoke thickly.

"I'll call—the clerk—thish ain't no way—to treat a—guesh—"

It was almost funny. His girly voice didn't go right—not for the drunk stuff. I swore at him.

"No good, Steiner—grab a chair; sit down. What were you after?"

He looked at me dumbly. I got sore. I got up, went over and hit him a hard one over the left ear. It knocked him to his knees.

"Come through—you dirty little rat!" I snapped. "What were you after?"

He looked helpless. But he went on with the bluff. "I'll call—the housh—detective—you can't—"

I tossed the gun on the bed—slashed out with my left.
Steiner swung back—stepped in close. I saw the right
coming up—it was a nasty punch. It came up through
my right arm—and I tried to ride with it. It didn't work.

My lower jaw clicked up—the end of my tongue caught
between my teeth. There was a lot of pain—and as I
started to go down, Steiner struck with his left. It landed.
My knees hit the floor. There was a stabbing pain along
my right side. Steiner's thin voice got out one, nasty
word. Then I was digging my head against the cheap
carpet—and forgetting a lot of things.

·5·

MISS McMURPHY

When I came out of it I got to my feet and looked around. Steiner was gone—and his gun was gone. The room was just about as it had been when he'd battered me down. He had a lot of strength for that kind of face.

I went into the bathroom and washed up. My tongue was in pretty bad shape—my jaw and the right side of my face were swollen. He'd kicked me in the right side. He was a dirty little rat—and he'd come out topside. That made me pretty sore.

I went down to the barbershop, told the man at the second chair that I'd walked into a door—and let the towels soak in for thirty minutes. I got some alcohol and rubbed my side. The bellhop brought me a quart and drank one with me. I downed two more, and in between I told myself what a damned fool I was. Then I packed the bag again. There wasn't anything missing. But Herb Steiner was out in the open—he'd been looking for something important.

I spent fifteen or twenty minutes holding cold water in my mouth, around my nicked tongue, and spitting it out. And I thought about Steiner while I did that. He wanted something he figured I had with me—and he wanted it pretty bad. I'd had him in a nice place—and then I'd acted dumb. That sort of thing wasn't going to pay.

"Steiner knew that Dot was rubbed out," I told myself. "He tried to give me a jolt—maybe he was figuring on coming after me later and, if I didn't come through, throwing a scare into me. Maybe not. Anyway, he stuck around up the river for three days after he got out. He thinks I've got something he wants—or someone else wants. He thinks I got it from Dot—"

I stopped muttering thickly and went out into the room again. I was beginning to feel pretty certain that Dot Ellis *had* had something important to say to me up the river. And I was beginning to feel pretty sure that one of the three murders hadn't been cheap.

I put the quart in the bag and went out of the room. My face hurt and my side ached. At the desk I checked out. The clerk stared at me.

"Walked into a door," I told him. "Just dumb."

He was sympathetic but suspicious. "That fellow named Herb—I forgot to tell you when I called up—he said he might be back later."

I took change for a twenty and tried out a grin. It hurt.

"Yeah," I returned, "he might be."

I got a cab and told the driver to take his time getting to the corner of Broadway and Fifty-sixth Street. My nerves were still kicking around—and Herb Steiner hadn't helped things any. I smoked a pill, got off at the right spot, and paid up.

At the boardinghouse where Wirt Donner had been murdered I rang the bell. The fat landlady looked as though she'd had good news. I stuck a foot across the sill for safety and got right to the point.

"A hundred dollars is a lot of money for the answers to a couple of questions," I told her. "You've got the answers—and I've got the questions and the hundred bucks."

She blinked a little. Her eyes were watery, and she looked as though she needed glasses. She smiled at me.

"Come on in," she said. "My feet is bad—they ain't been right since—"

"I haven't got much time," I cut in. "Let's make it a private talk."

She took me into a combination parlor and bedroom, in which everything was faded and odorous. She sat on a sofa and I took a chair that had a lot of gilt on it.

"You may remember me," I said. "You told Donelly I looked like your sister's first husband—the night Donner had stomach trouble."

She rocked a little from side to side on the sofa. She kept on smiling.

"You're a detective," she announced.

I nodded. "But not a copper," I told her. "Got an agency of my own—work alone, see?"

She had a hoarse laugh. "Just like Sherlock Holmes," she stated.

She had me guessing. I couldn't figure her—a wise lady—or dumb? So I gave her the benefit of the doubt, rated her dumb.

"About the same," I said. "You know that Red Salmon shot Donner."

She laughed again. "Like hell he did!" she announced.

I got up from the chair. Things weren't going so good. There were curtains at one end of the room, and I strolled around, passed the pills, lighted one for her, picked a chair that faced the curtains.

"Wirt Donner was a pretty good guy," I said. "Maybe Red didn't get him. I'd sort of like to know."

The landlady nodded her head. "Red didn't," she said, "and I didn't tell you I knew who did, did I?"

I unscrambled the "dids" and shook my head.

"You told me that the tall lady who lived here had gone to Pittsburgh—to visit her aunt. I think you said the aunt's name was Munn. You said the tall lady's name was Bock—Ella Bock. I'll be frank, Mrs.—"

"Miss McMurphy," she finished for me. "And like hell you'll be frank!"

I looked at the curtains and decided that maybe the wind was blowing through from the rear of the house somewhere—and making them move. I said: "Are you interested in my hundred—or not?"

"You're damn tootin' I am!" she replied, and put a lot of feeling into the words. "But you've got to play straight."

I nodded. "I'm not going to hurt Ella Bock," I said. "Maybe I know as much about all this as you do—maybe not. One thing is sure, I'll know if you're lying."

She looked pained. She stopped rocking from side to side, shoved some stringy hair back on top of her head.

"Ask the two questions," she said. "If you don't like the answers—hang on to your coin."

That sounded fair enough. I asked the first one.

"The woman is around forty, sharp face, nose—features. Has blond hair—black underneath the chemical. Dopey eyes. She yelled when Mike Donelly grabbed her. You called her Ella Bock, but that isn't her name. I want to be sure we get the right person."

The fat one smiled a little. "You ain't asking questions," she told me.

I grinned. "The woman was living here with Wirt Donner, wasn't she?" I asked.

The landlady started to rock again. She nodded. "Yeah," she replied.

I asked the other one right away. "What's her real name?"

The landlady hesitated. "Virgie Beers," she said. "And that's the truth."

I smiled. "That's where you got the 'Bock,' " I said. "What's the first name for—Virgin?"

I let her have the laugh. She had her whole body in it.

Hell, no!" she came back. "Virgie—Virginia. Virginia Beers."

I handed her two fifties—and she swore a few times as she fingered the bills. Then I took out a third fifty.

"I'm not going to hurt Virgie, Miss McMurphy. You gave me two answers, and I trusted you. I handed you the money. Now I want you to trust me. Give me Virgie's address in Pittsburgh. If she's there when I get there— I'll mail you the fifty."

The landlady eyed me narrowly. "When'll you get there?" she asked.

"Tomorrow," I replied.

She got up with an effort. "I'll write it down for you," she said.

"Never mind—I'll remember it." I watched her eyes get to be little slits. "I've got a nice memory."

"It's a steel-mill town," she told me. "Duquesne." She spelled it laboriously. "The number is Seven thirty-six, Second Street. It's about forty minutes outside of Pittsburgh."

I nodded. "Want to tell me anything else—for nothing?" I asked. "I'm broke."

"Virgie's a good kid," she said. "She ain't forty— like you said. Virgie's all right. She ain't got no breaks, that's all. I wouldn't want to see her hurt."

I waited. The landlady looked as though if she got started she might go on. She was frowning.

"Red was framed," she said. "I guess you know that. Say, who are you working for—Babe?"

I didn't like the tone of her voice. She was getting suspicious now. In a couple of minutes she might begin to figure she'd made a mistake.

"Babe who?" I asked.

She tightened up. "Donner had a friend named Babe," she said. "A male. He had dough. I figured he might be sore."

I told her that maybe I was working for Babe, and that there would be fifty coming from Duquesne in a couple of days if she'd given me a good number. She brightened up a little—said that was all she knew, anyway. We headed for the door.

"Where did Donner get shot?" I asked her.

"In the stomach," she said, and opened the door.

I told her that I meant in what part of the house, and she said she'd been sleeping and didn't know about the shots. And that her feet were hurting so bad she thought she'd take a nap right away.

I told her that was a good idea and went down the steps. Donelly came across the street, grinned at me.

"Just luck," he said cheerfully. "Did you get the information?"

I started to tell him something that wouldn't mean much—and he widened his eyes on my face.

"You've been fighting again!" he said. "Is that nice? What'll your grandfather up in Boston say?"

"He won't mind," I answered. "He's been broad-minded since his hundredth birthday."

Donelly looked up the steps of the boardinghouse.

"Anybody home?" he asked.

I shook my head. "I tried a long while—but I couldn't get in."

The red-faced dick nodded. "You came *out* without any trouble, though," he said. "See you later!"

I said I hoped not and went over toward Broadway. Thirty minutes later I was in Jersey—and in another hour I was flying over that state. The transport plane was heading for Pittsburgh. I knew the city—and I knew Duquesne. A steel-mill town not boasting much about its population of twelve thousand foreigners and two thousand Americans.

The fat landlady had said something that helped a lot. And she hadn't been paid for saying it. She'd asked me if I were working for "Babe." And Ben Garren had told me, as we listened to that voice coming over the radio in his flat, that Cherulli had been playing Babe Mullens— "a big nice-lined moll." She had come out of Harlem, he'd said—"to the glitter spots."

I sat back in the wicker chair, closed my eyes, listened to the beat of the three engines, and thought back. Things were clearing up a bit. But not too much. My guess was that Dot Ellis had come up the river to see me for a real reason. Cherulli wasn't dead when she'd come up—but maybe she'd had a hunch. She'd had something with her—and Ben Garren had got it. Something important. That was the way I figured it. Herb Steiner thought I'd got whatever Dot had, but he hadn't thought it until after Garren had been pumped out. He hadn't stayed close enough to me coming down the river.

Wirt Donner had told me about this blond woman, up in the Big House. I hadn't been guessing when I'd sprung the question on Miss McMurphy. And Virgie Beers had gone over to Ben Garren's flat—pretty quickly after Donner had been finished. Virgie knew things—and I wanted to chat with her. If I got close enough—we'd chat. There was an even chance.

2

There were floodlights on the field outside of Pittsburgh when the transport plane landed. Red flames streaked up into the sky from the plant stacks. Red smoke hung low. The air was heavy, thick with steel grime. I caught a cab for the Seventh Avenue Hotel. It wasn't the best in the city—nor the worst. After some food I went down to the editorial rooms of the *Post-Dispatch*.

They'd moved them up a few floors since I'd worked on the sheet, seven or eight years ago, but they were just as dirty as ever. I walked between a lot of cigarette-scarred desks holding ancient typewriters, saw Phil Dobe look up from the city desk and spot me.

"Holy Jesus!" he shouted. "It's Mal Ourney!"

We shook hands. Phil had been a feature writer when I'd worked the hotel beat. He was older and heavier, and his teeth were pretty bad. Otherwise he hadn't changed.

"When'd you get out?" he asked.

I told him. He grinned at me, swore fervently.

"What a dumb newshound you *would* have turned out to be!" he stated. "Taking two years for a tart who was so rotten she tried to grab graft coin from the wop she was livin' with—and who got the works!"

I stared at Dobe. He had small, dark eyes and a barrel chest. He spoke right out, and he said what he thought. He wasn't always right, but he was always sure.

"What graft coin—and what wop?" I asked.

Phil Dobe took his eyes away from me and shouted at a redheaded reporter who was dropping cigarette ashes over the keys of a typewriter and working hard with two fingers. The city editor was howling about the deadline—they were getting right up on it. He looked at me again.

"Where you been?" he stated. "You mean you don't know about the two hundred grand?"

I shook my head. Dobe pointed toward the telegraph desk. He shouted across the noisy room.

"Oh, Red—give Ourney the Cherulli follow-up, will you?"

I went over to the telegraph desk and a redhaired gent in a blue shirt and a yellow tie handed me some yellow stuff just off the machine. It had a New York dateline. The idea was that Babe Mullens claimed that someone had grabbed two hundred thousand in cold cash from Cherulli, before he'd been rubbed out. She suspected a lot of people. And she wasn't making any secret of it. Dot Ellis got most of the publicity. Ben Garren came in for some, and so did Wirt Donner. My name wasn't mentioned, and neither was Herb Steiner's. The Babe claimed that Cherulli owed her fifty thousand. She was yelling wide open to get it.

I read the stuff twice, handed it back to the redheaded gent, and walked around to the city desk. The fire alarm banged out, and Phil Dobe swore.

"Second!" he muttered. "Up in the Hill district. Oh, Danny—hop up and if it's a prosty joint we'll get a funny box on it."

A copyreader I'd never seen before went on using his pencil and observed that if it was that sort of a joint Joe Burns might be getting his hair singed. Dobe grinned and said that even though it was Joe's day off he wasn't up in the Hill district. He was over at the *News-Press* trying to kid Cryson into giving him a two-dollar raise and a job. It wouldn't work because Dobe had got to Cryson first and had told him that Joe was sober only three days a week. He was damn good when he was sober.

Dobe tilted back his chair and looked me over.

"Two hundred grand is a lot of coin," he stated. "What you doin' with it, Mal?"

I swore. "It's a lot of money—even if Cherulli never had it," I stated. "But where does the story come in— for you?"

The city editor grunted. "That wop was one of our most respected citizens, about five years ago. You don't remember him, Mal. He was managing that heavy— Dinah Reese. Reese got the Dinah from dynamite. He slugged Cherulli out one day, and that started him peddling the liquid stuff. Made coin and pulled out. Tried the racket in New York. He was lucky."

I nodded. "Until a couple of days ago—he was," I stated.

The city editor grinned. "Why the honor?" he asked. "Looking for a job?"

I shook my head. "How about a gal named Virgie Beers?" I asked. "Ever hear of her?"

Dobe grinned. "It's a hell of a name," he stated. "And I'd remember it—but I don't. What about her?"

I shook my head. "Not for publication," I told him. "Virginia Beers, it is."

The city editor shook his head. "If you're going to kill her, let me send a photographer along," he urged.

I grinned. We were both thinking. Dobe got there first.

"Maybe you figure she's got the two hundred grand?" he suggested.

I laughed that off. "I don't figure Cherulli ever had it," I stated.

"The hell you don't!" Dobe wasn't grinning. "I've been reading the papers, Mal. You're mixed up in this like juniper-juice in alcohol. You get around."

That sounded familiar. I told Dobe that I was just trying to do a gal a good turn, and that it wasn't important.

"Sure," he agreed. "Keep it up and you'll get the Eagle badge. How about drinking with me tonight, after 'thirty'?"

I shook my head. "Maybe tomorrow night," I told him. "I'm hitting the hay for—"

A phone bell rang and Dobe lifted a receiver. He listened for thirty seconds, said "yes" once and "no" twice, hung up. He grinned at me.

"Murder in Duquesne," he stated. "Cheap stuff—down the hill. Too close to the mill. All the officials live up high. This one was on Second Street."

I tried to look dumb. Dobe reached for a cigar. Second Street—Duquesne. I asked a question.

"Male or female?"

Dobe grinned. "Female," he stated. "District man's on his way out there to try and swipe a picture. Probably some plant hunky got a cinder in his eye and came home off shift. Got out the ax and chopped up the wife. That's the way it's still being done, Mal."

I nodded. "See you tomorrow," I told him. "I'm going to bed."

Dobe said that maybe I was.

Outside the newspaper office I figured the quickest way to get to Duquesne would be in a cab. I hailed one. The driver looked so much like the bird that had driven Dot Ellis on her last trip that it gave me the jumps.

"Riding in cabs bothers me," I told him. "Give me a break—and miss things by more than a foot."

"I ain't killed a guy for three months," he told me. "And then it was his fault. He was drunker than me."

I nodded and told him to take me to Second Street, Duquesne.

·6·

MILL TOWN

On the way to the mill town I decided a few things. One was that Babe Mullens had talked big figures. The other was that there had been a steal of cash—big cash. But not two hundred thousand. Maybe fifty grand—maybe seventy-five. It had been Cherulli's coin, or he had been passing it along. Someone had grabbed it. Then the killings had started. And finally Herb Steiner had figured me so dumb that I'd pack the coin in a bag.

I didn't like the last thought so much. Didn't figure that Steiner would rate me that way. But I was pretty sure that Lentz had known some coin was missing when he'd sent for me. And Steiner had been down to the Headquarters office, too.

My tongue felt a little better—but it was pretty swollen. My face wasn't so bad. Steiner had been tricky—and I'd have to get him right the next time—or not at all.

The cab was getting outside of Pittsburgh, climbing the grade beyond the Pennsylvania Station. I could look around and see the sky tinted with red—and smoke drifting. There were mills along the rivers, close to the city.

I had about fifty minutes to think—and at the end of that time, as the cab neared Duquesne, it hadn't done me much good. The Duquesne plant showed down the river as the cab crossed a bridge, then followed along near the bank. Things became murkier—smoke drifted out from the mill, toward the town that sprawled up the hill. The driver jerked his head and asked me what part of Second Street. I thought of the address Miss Mc-Murphy had given me—736.

"Where's the police station up here?" I asked.

The driver didn't know, but a fat cop standing on a corner a few squares along gave us the dope. It was almost eleven o'clock, but the town looked busy as we crossed the main street, which ran up from the plant—up the hill. The mill worked three shifts, and the workers going on the job in an hour were out and stirring. They were a tough-looking bunch.

The police station was two blocks up the hill, and just off the main street. I paid too much money, told the driver I wouldn't need him anymore, and went into the station. A lean-faced cop sat behind a low rail and frowned at me. He was smoking a corncob pipe, and the room was filled with odor.

"I'm Higgins, from the *Post-Dispatch*," I told him. "Murder on Second Street—and we got the address garbled, down at the paper."

He took the stem of the corncob from between a flock of pretty good teeth, spat with noise, and muttered something I didn't get. Then he spoke more clearly. "What kind of a murder?"

I grinned at him. "That's what I came up to find out," I said.

"Yeah?"

He put the pipe back in his face again, picked up a magazine, and started to read. I told him that I knew Duquesne was a steel-mill town, and that the officials didn't like newspaper men. I told him that he might never have seen me before, but that I wasn't a cub reporter getting my first story. I said that if he didn't want to talk I'd take a look at the blotter. He set the magazine down and leaned forward from his chair.

"I'll give you ten to one you won't look at no blotter!" he snapped.

I was getting sore, but I didn't show it. My bluff wasn't going so good—I didn't know who was who in the town and couldn't play it that way.

"What the hell's the idea?" I demanded. "Did the paper keep your face out of the pages the time you went after a hunky with nothing but a gun and a blackjack in your hands?"

He got up from the chair, tossed the magazine to one side, and put two big hands on his hips. He was big and hard.

"Get moving out of here!" he snapped. "I'm Kellar— and no paper men tell me what to do and what not to do!"

I looked at him a little and decided he was right. A short, fat fellow came in through the door.

"Where's Jim?" he asked the copper. "Up at the Widow's place?"

The copper swore at the short man, and I went outside, walked toward the main street, went into a combination poolroom and cigar store, and picked out a pale-faced man who seemed to be running things.

"Is the Widow still sleeping at Seven thirty-six Second Street?" I asked, smiling.

The pale-faced one grunted. "Widow Gunsten?" he muttered. "Her place is at Seven thirty-four, ain't it?"

I nodded. "Knew it was up there somewhere," I said. "Thanks."

It took me five minutes to get out to 734 Second Street. The street was narrow, dirty. Mill smoke drifted over it. Mill sound reached it clearly. The clatter of rolls grinding white-hot, thick ingots into thin ingots. The hiss of steam—

the clang of overhead cranes. The street was filled with sound.

Seven thirty-four was an ore-stained, frame house, small and sagging. I went past it, looked at 736. There wasn't much difference in the two, except that the place whose address Miss McMurphy had given me was set back a little farther from the cracked sidewalk. It didn't have a yard—there was just some dirt in front of the house. There was a light in the back—the front rooms were dark.

I walked back to 734. The place was lighted up like Roxy's theater lobby. Every room had a light. The front was open, and behind dirty, stained shades I could see the outline of figures. I went toward the front door—a man came out and stood on the porch, lighting a cigarette.

He was young and white—and he had a soft hat shoved back on his head. I made a guess.

"You the *Post-Dispatch* district man?"

He nodded. "I'm Grady."

"I'm Higgins," I told him. "New man at the paper. Dobe said you were on the way here. What is it?"

He swore. "Some guy used a knife on the Widow," he stated. "Fancy work—she's all cut into figure eights."

"Yeah?" I said. "I'm from Cleveland—the *Press*. Who's the Widow?"

He looked superior. The light from inside let me see that.

"Nellie Gunsten," he stated. "Runs three speaks in town—loans money to the bohunks. Used to be a stock actress—long time ago. Dunning one of the Poles for the coin she'd loaned, maybe. And he carved her."

"Get away?" I asked.

He nodded. "Chief Butman says he knows something," he stated. "But he always says that—and nothing much ever happens. Who'd they fire at the paper?"

I told him nobody—that they were just taking on a few stray reporters. He didn't seem to believe that. I went inside the house. The Widow was lying in the kitchen. The place was a mess inside, but she looked worse than the house. There were a lot of men around, but they didn't seem to be doing much except lighting cigarettes.

A man with a lot of gold teeth and a derby he kept tapping against his knee announced that it was a "dirty shame." Several others agreed. No one paid much attention to me. I went out through the back door, saw a break in a wire fence that separated the two houses I was interested in, and walked through it.

The light I'd seen from the front of 736 was in the kitchen. I went up two steps, tapped on a screen door. An inside door opened and a red-haired woman of about fifty showed me a homely face.

"I'd like to ask—"

She cut in with a tinny tone, and her thin lips didn't move much.

"No one livin' here killed her—an' we don't know nothin' about it. We told all we know to Butman—"

She started to shut the door, but I got my foot in the way. I stuck my head in close and had my say sharply.

"I'm not interested in the Widow—I'm from New York, and Herb Steiner told me to look up Virgie Beers."

The red-haired woman's lower jaw sagged. She took her hands away from the door and backed up. I went in, shutting the door behind me.

"If any bulls come in while I'm here—I'm Higgins," I advised. "Reporter on the *Post-Dispatch*—a new man. Does that sink in?"

She said it did. A door slammed somewhere upstairs. The red-haired woman jumped around like a trained flea. I grinned at her.

"You've got nerves," I said. "Where's Virgie?"

She swore hoarsely and went out of the kitchen. I picked out a stool and sat down on it, lighting a pill. There were stairs at the front of the house, and they didn't have any carpet on them. I could hear the red-haired one going up. After a while I heard someone else coming down. The steps had a lighter sound under this one's weight.

Virgie came in. She looked tired—she had circles under the eyes. She looked older than she had in the boardinghouse in New York. A white bulb in the kitchen didn't help her blond hair any. Her nose didn't look as thin as it had before, but her eyes looked as dopey. She stopped in the hall just outside the door, looked me over.

I got up and grinned.

"Remember? I came in with Donelly. Donner was down at the bottom of the steps—"

That was as far as I got. She sucked in some air, took a step forward, went down on her knees. I stopped her before she went the rest of the way, dragged her over to the chair I'd been sitting on. She was making funny strangling noises. Her face was white.

I went over to the sink and ran some cold water on my handkerchief. When the cloth touched her face it seemed to help a little. She closed her eyes and stopped making the noises.

"Sorry," I said. "Did I say the wrong thing—or were you feeling this way anyway?"

She shook her head a little. After a while she sat up. "I'm all right. You're Ourney—how'd you find me?"

She had a rather nice voice. It didn't sound the way it had in the Fifty-sixth Street boardinghouse. I told her the truth.

"Paid Miss McMurphy some hat money—told her I wouldn't hurt you. She believed me, maybe."

Virgie nodded her head and showed a faint smile.

"Maybe," she agreed.

I suggested that we get out of the kitchen, get somewhere we might not be interrupted. She sat up, shivered a little, stood up. I gave her a hand and we went into a small parlor. It was dark—but she told me where the light was. I switched it on. It was a dim one—sort of greenish. The shades of the room were down.

Virgie went over and took it easy on a couch. She lay on her back and looked up at a dirty-colored ceiling. She looked all in.

"I'll be naïve—and ask you a question that may sound that way," I told her.

She shook her head. "It's a two-dollar word—that 'naïve,' " she said. "Talk so I can understand."

I nodded. "Wirt Donner struck me as being white," I said. "I trusted him, up the river. He told me a lot— and it went pretty deep. I got the idea that just a few humans were using a lot of other humans as they wanted, then framing them, smashing them—rubbing them out. It looked pretty rotten to me. I'm not sentimental—I'm curious. I'd like to smash some of the ones who use the others up. I talked it over with Wirt—he gave me a bum steer on a human he called a 'good guy.' Maybe you know about that."

She looked at me, turning her head a little.

"About what?" she asked.

"About Ben Garren," I said.

She shook her head. "Never heard of him," she said.

I got up and walked around a little. Then I sat down again.

"All right, Virgie," I said. "But you're a damned fool for lying. They'll get you just the way they got Dot—and Wirt Donner. You won't have a chance. If you play square with me—something may happen."

She laughed harshly. There was a little silence.

"What makes you think I'm lying?" she asked finally.

"Saw you go into Ben's flat," I said grimly. "Heard you talking inside. The radio wasn't loud enough. You were a little hysterical—Donner had only been dead an hour or so."

She said: "Oh, God," in a flat tone. I fed her a little more truth.

"They grabbed Red Salmon—third-degreed a confession, and let him die on them. For some reason it suited all right. But Red never got Wirt Donner. I chased you out here to ask you one important question. It's the one I spoke about a few minutes ago. Who got Wirt?"

She said very calmly: "I don't know."

I believed her. There wasn't any particular reason for it, but I believed her.

"Listen—" I said—"I'm trying to make you see that I think Wirt was going square. Something went wrong, before I could get to him. He talked about you, in the Big House. When I saw you I recognized you. Miss McMurphy said you were living with him."

She sat up, swung her feet to the floor, pulled a blue dress down over pretty nice knees, and drew in her breath.

"Damn McMurphy!"

I leaned over and grabbed the material of her dress, just under her neck. I pulled her toward me a few inches.

"What did you shoot Wirt for?" I gritted at her.

She pulled back, lifted her right hand, and struck me sharply across the face. It stung, but I hung on.

"You lived with him!" I snapped. "You murdered him! And then you went to Ben Garren and cried about it!"

She tried to hit me again, but I got my left arm in the way.

"You're a dirty liar!" she shrilled. "I didn't—shoot him—"

I pulled her face closer to mine and got a lot of feeling in my voice. "You ducked the big town—you came out here. Why?"

"I didn't want—to get pulled in!" She was almost screaming now. "The bulls were all over the place—"

Someone was pounding at the back door. I let her go. It was a tough break, because I wasn't hurting her any— and I was getting close.

"I'm Higgins—*Post-Dispatch* reporter," I told her. "What happened next door—before I let this guy in?"

She dropped down on the sofa, shook her head.

"I didn't—kill Wirt!" she half sobbed.

I was coming close to believing that one, too. There were steps on the stairs—the red-haired woman was coming down. I went out and met her near the kitchen. Her eyes were narrowed.

"Lay off Virgie!" she warned. "She's been mauled enough."

I went out and opened the door. It wasn't locked. Grady frowned at me.

"What's up?" he asked. "Got anything?"

I shook my head. "Just seeing if the Widow's neighbors know anything," I told him. "They don't."

Grady looked at me suspiciously. He spoke in a flat voice.

"Butman wants to see you—next door."

I nodded. "Through in a minute," I said. "Just trying to pick up a feature story. Tell him I'll be right over."

He went outside and I went back into the parlor. The red-haired woman followed me in. She wore a blue negligee, and her right hand was hidden in the folds of it. Virgie Beers was lying on the sofa again, on her back. She had her eyes closed, but she opened them as I came up close and looked down at her.

"I'm tired as hell," she said tonelessly. "Maybe you're all right—I don't know. I don't care much. Ask 'em—I'll try and answer."

"Who killed Donner?" I asked.

She closed her eyes and shook her head. Her voice was unsteady.

"I don't know. If I did I'd go out and get him myself. Wirt was a good—guy."

I believed her. But I didn't let her know it.

"Why was he murdered?" I asked.

She hesitated a second. Then she spoke in a low voice. "They thought he had the hundred grand," she said.

"What hundred grand?" I came back.

She opened her eyes, but they were expressionless.

"The stuff Cherulli was passing on up," she said. "It got missing, on the way. I suppose you don't know that? A hundred grand."

I looked toward the door that led into the kitchen. Babe Mullens had called it two hundred.

"And Wirt didn't have it?" I kept on.

Her voice had a savage note. "He never saw it!" she said. "He was waiting for you—and he wouldn't listen to me. I told him he was a fool. I told him to get clear. But he was sticking around, waiting for you!"

I nodded. "Garren swore he didn't know you," I told her. "You went to his flat. Where did he come in?"

"I knew him before he did the last stretch." Her voice was flat again. "About a week ago he sent for Donner. Wirt wouldn't go. I wouldn't let him. The dicks were watching Ben, and he was in with Cherulli. Then Ben sent me word that if I didn't get Wirt over to his place it would be just too bad. I begged Wirt to make a break— it looked rotten. He was waiting for you. Said you and he were going to do something that was right, something decent. Wouldn't tell me any more. Then they got him— and I went to Ben to tell him what I thought. He laughed at me. Said if I yelped he'd frame me—"

Her voice broke. She had the fingers of her right hand over her eyes. I put a cigarette in them, lighted up.

"We would have done—something decent," I told her. "Maybe it can be done yet. Are you square with me?"

She let me see her eyes. "I swear to Christ I am!" she said.

"One more—then I'll go over and let Butman talk," I said. "What happened next door?"

"It doesn't count," she said. "Some mill worker did it."

I nodded, told her to take it easy and that I'd be back pretty quick. I went past the red-haired woman and gave her a grin.

"Look out that gun doesn't go off in the folds of your dress and send a bullet through your fanny," I advised.

She said it was her gun and her fanny, and that if I didn't like it I could go places.

·7·

BUTMAN

I met Grady on the back porch, and he said Chief Butman
was looking for me.

"Anything new?" I asked.

Grady dropped a butt, stepped on it.

"He figures he's got the carver," he said. "Someone
called up and said to trace a lady named Virgie Beers,
on from New York. Butman's been poking around in
drawers—and he's found a threatening note. Signed by
this Beers woman. It looks like an out."

I nodded, fumbled in my pocket, said I'd left my stub
of a pencil inside. I went back in and gave Virgie and
the red-haired woman the news. Virgie sat up and looked
scared. Then she looked mad. She said it was a frame.
She'd only spoken a few words to the Widow in her life.
She'd never written her. She didn't know anything more
about her than was mill-town rumor. She hadn't been in
Duquesne for six months until this trip.

"Don't be here now," I suggested. "And make it fast
getting out. Go in to Pittsburgh and register at the Gurly
House as Mrs. Howard Evans. Stay in your room. I may
call you up later tonight—or I may not. Need money?"

She said no, and I headed toward the kitchen again. She was getting up—and the red-haired woman looked at me.

"What do I do?" she asked.

"Drop out of sight if you want to live quietly," I replied. "Stay here and double-cross Virgie if you're dumb enough to figure it would be a good idea."

She swore at me as I went into the kitchen. I didn't figure she'd double-cross Virgie. Outside I headed for the other house. Butman had his derby on and was coming toward the break in the fence.

"I'm Higgins," I told him. "Grady said you wanted to talk with me."

He grunted. He showed his gold teeth in a smile that wasn't a smile.

"You've been walkin' all over the place," he stated. "Why didn't you talk to me first?"

"I'm not after the facts," I told him. "Phil Dobe sent me up to get a feature story—sob stuff, maybe. Did the Widow have a canary bird that won't have anyone to feed it anymore?"

Butman had nasty eyes. They slanted a little, and they had a cold expression in them. They were gray.

"You've been over next door. Did the Donner woman talk?"

That was a surprise, but it was fairly dark and I figured he hadn't seen enough to make much difference.

"What Donner woman?" I stalled.

Butman swore. "The redheaded one," he stated. "Sister of the yegg that was murdered in New York—ever read the papers?"

I felt better. Butman was telling me things.

"I don't have to read 'em—just write 'em," I stated. "The red-haired lady said she hadn't even heard a yelp next door. There was no story for me, so I didn't get her name."

Butman took off his derby, tapped it against his right

knee, looked toward the lights in the kitchen of the Donner residence.

"I'll go in and maybe her memory'll get better," he muttered.

"If you get rough enough," I said, "that'll be my feature story. 'Chief of Duquesne police force beats up red-haired sister of New York yegg because she didn't hear the Widow yelp as she was being carved by mysterious murderer!' Good?"

Butman stuck his face close to mine and told me that I was a new man so far as Duquesne was concerned, and that it wasn't wise to be funny with him. He said that he was a hard guy, and that the guys under him were hard. He said that he didn't like newspaper reporters, and that Duquesne was one steel-mill town that could do without them.

I wanted to keep him out of the Donner place for a couple more minutes, and I tried to figure how sore I could get him without going all the way.

"The *Post-Dispatch* has a nice circulation up here," I told him. "It wouldn't hurt you any to get your name smeared around as being a good man."

He laughed at that, showing all the gold.

"It wouldn't do me any good, either," he stated. "I'll get my publicity in the Duquesne *News*—my brother runs it."

I grinned. "Have it your own way," I told him. "Mind if I stick around?"

He grunted. "If you do," he told me, "you'll get what I want to give you—and that's all."

I offered him a cigarette, and he turned it down. He went toward the Donner house, with Grady following. I called out to him as he reached the two steps of the back porch.

"Oh, Chief—do you figure this has anything to do with those killings in New York?"

I called out pretty loudly, figuring that if Virgie and

the Donner woman weren't out of the house they'd get out in a hurry. Butman came down from the steps, talking to himself. I met him at the break in the fence. His face was twisted.

"Keep your loud mouth shut!" he gritted, his face close to mine. "What I figure I'll keep to myself. Any more wisecracks from you and I'll run you out of town."

I looked hurt. "But I just wanted to know—"

He called me a name, swung around and went into the Donner house. I lighted another pill. Virgie hadn't had much time, but maybe she'd had enough. I walked around to the front of the Widow's house. A cab pulled up and a round-shouldered chap got out. He told the driver to wait.

"Where's the body?" he asked me. "I'm Spencer, from the *Post-Dispatch*."

I told him where the body was, and he went around back. I walked over and stood beside the cab driver.

"You just brought Al out here," I told him. "He hasn't paid up yet. I'm from another paper, and I've got what I want. I'm in a hurry to get back to Pittsburgh. I'll slip you twenty right now—for the trip back."

The driver grinned. "Slide in!" he told me.

I got in, handed him twenty through the window, dropped back on the seat. I saw Butman come out through the front door of the Donner place as the cab jerked forward. He was swearing, and looking around. He yelled at the cab, but the driver just grinned at me—and let her pick up speed.

He drove down Second—and I told him to cross Main and keep on going. There was no sign of Virgie Beers or the Donner woman. But they knew shortcuts, maybe. I looked around—and the lights of a car were shining in my face. The car was gaining on the cab. Gaining fast.

"Slow down, pull into the curb!" I ordered the driver.

The other car slid up, stopped beside the cab. Butman climbed down from behind the wheel.

"What's the rush?" he demanded.

I grinned at him. "Hunting for a phone. Got to call the paper."

He smiled back—that nasty smile of his. He had a mocking tone in his voice.

"How about the phone in the Widow's house?" he asked.

I kept on grinning. "It's a long-distance call," I said. "Hate to run up a bill on her heirs."

"Get out of the cab—and climb in with me!" he ordered. "I'm thinking up some questions to ask you."

I got out, told the driver to follow us, and climbed in beside him. He drove up past the Widow's house, but he didn't stop. He turned to the right, started the car up a steep hill in low. Then he pulled in at the curb. When the cab driver pulled up beside the car he got his head over the door.

"Go back to the house where you dropped the passenger you brought up," he ordered. "Wait there—and, say, did you bring this bird out?"

The cab driver was frowning. "Who wants to know?" he demanded.

Butman told him. The cab driver changed his tone. He said he didn't bring me out, and he volunteered the information that I'd given him twenty for the trip back to Pittsburgh. Butman told him to keep the twenty and to drive back to the Widow's place and wait.

He shifted into low—and climbed on up the hill. The street became a road that wound a lot. It wasn't a very good road. The steel mill sprawled along the river for a mile or so, far below. Red smoke hung over it.

Butman was driving with a grin on his face. I asked some questions and he answered them grimly. The road leveled off—we drove past a cemetery. The houses were thinning out—and there wasn't any traffic. I told Butman that he was going pretty far.

"About five miles more!" he said. "It won't be a bad walk."

"It's a dirty trick, just the same," I said. "There'll be hell to pay—when I get back to the paper."

He chuckled hoarsely. "We're used to hot stuff out here," he stated. "I could give you the works—and get away with it."

"What for?" I asked.

"Trying to run things your way," he replied.

He stopped the car after about a mile. There weren't any houses around, but there were a lot of trees. He backed, went forward, backed again. Then he got turned around.

"Slide out!" he ordered. "Keep away from the Widow's place when you get back. And remember, *I'm* running this man's town!"

I slid out. And I kept my eyes on the car. Butman shifted, jerked the car forward. It was an open car, with a black top. It was dark in color. I watched it pick up speed—then it rounded a turn. The taillight faded. I swore softly. My guess was that I'd have a five-mile walk to the cemetery, and that was on the outskirts of the town.

Time didn't count much. It was the walk that bothered me. I started moving. Butman figured I was a dumb newspaperman. He figured he could do a lot of things before I got back. He figured he was teaching me a lesson. That gave me a laugh. Virgie and the red-haired sister of Wirt Donner would be in the clear. Butman had been hurting his own chances.

I walked along the side of the road. It wasn't a black night—there were a lot of stars. And the sky was tinted red—over the steel plant beyond. I thought about Virgie—decided to believe her. The redheaded woman was Wirt Donner's sister—and Virgie Beers had come to her place. Cherulli had been passing along a hundred grand—and it had been grabbed. Virgie didn't know who had murdered Donner. She had suspected Ben Garren, and that was why I'd seen her at the flat. The Widow's death didn't count.

I wasn't so sure about that. But something was on—something important. I was stringing along with cheap crooks, but one hundred thousand dollars wasn't cheap crooks' coin. They were being used, handled. When things went right they got a break. When things went wrong they got rubbed out, or framed. The big boys gave the orders.

Someone had tried to frame Virgie Beers for the murder of the Widow. Salmon had been framed for the kill of Wirt Donner. A wreck from drugs, he had passed out of the picture. If he'd lived he wouldn't have had a chance. Dot Ellis and Wirt Donner—their killer or killers had reasons. A hundred grand was a lot of coin.

"I wanted to scrap this way," I muttered as I walked along the road. "And whether I wanted to or not—they were watching me. Maybe they tried to frame me for Dot's finish—and it didn't take. Maybe—"

I stopped talking to myself. There was the distant squeal of brakes. They seemed to come from the road, somewhere beyond the turn. There was a little silence—then a single shot. Right on top of it there sounded the staccato beat of a gun—a machine gun. It was regular until the sound broke. Then it sounded again. Then silence.

I ran toward the bend, but before I turned it I got off the road, into the low growth at the right side. There was a level stretch beyond the curve, for perhaps the distance of two city squares. Then another curve. I couldn't see anything on the road, so I got back on and walked fast. When I reached the next curve I got off to the side again. There were no more sounds—not even the hum of a car's engine.

The machine was half a city square beyond the second curve. It was slanted to one side—to the left side of the road. Three red lanterns had been set across the road. I walked through the low growth until I got up close. It was the car that Butman had driven.

No one was around but the Duquesne chief of police. He was slumped across the wheel—the engine of the car was still running. The gear lever was in neutral—the emergency brake was on. The windshield was shattered—and the whole car was torn with bullets. Butman had a few in his head, a lot in his chest. His gun lay near his feet.

His derby was in the back of the car, and a cigar was lying on the seat beside him. It was lighted and burning the upholstery. Both of Butman's eyes were open, but his mouth was closed. Any one of a half-dozen bullets would have killed him.

I walked away from the car and looked at the three red lanterns. They hadn't been there fifteen minutes ago, when Butman had driven me over this stretch. Someone had seen us pass—or someone had followed. The lantern in the center of the road was smoking—the wicks of the other two were all right. I couldn't see any tracks of tires that looked important. The dirt was hard packed.

I let the cigar burn the upholstery, and the engine keep on running. I walked on toward the town and the red color hanging over it. I began to think that Virgie Beers was telling considerable truth. A hundred thousand— that was important money. Mistakes were bad business. It looked as though Chief Butman had made one.

·8·

GREEN ICE

It was twelve twenty when I got out of a cab a square from the *Post-Dispatch* building. There was a café near the paper, and I looked in cautiously, hoping that I'd see Phil Dobe eating some pie and downing some java. I had a bag checked up in his office, and I wanted to get it without a lot of talk. But I didn't see him.

He was at his desk when I came into the editorial room, his feet propped up in front of him. He was reading a book and chewing something. A few reporters were around, but it looked a lot as though "thirty" had come in. I got around behind him and peeped at the book's title: *Extraordinary Women*. While I was looking at it Phil spoke.

"You lying bum—what was the game you were playing up at Duquesne?"

I sat down on the desk surface, shoving his feet off.

"Who sprayed that chief of police so he won't talk anymore?" I asked.

The city editor swore. "I said you get around, and hell—I mean it!" he stated. "How'd you know Butman was finished off?"

I grinned. "Heard it in town, just before I came down," I told him. "But I didn't hear who carved up the Widow."

Dobe swallowed the stuff he was chewing, tossed the book on the desk, and glared at me.

"You went up there and mixed in," he said. "You passed off as one of my men. They phoned in and described you. Why in hell—"

"Tell me who did for Butman and the Widow, and I'll tell you something else," I said. "It might be news— and it might not."

Dobe grunted. "It probably wouldn't," he returned. "Butman and the Widow had been good pals. She wasn't much to look at, but there's no accounting for some guys' tastes. About a week ago he fell for a Polish girl, working in the steel plant's General Office up there. The Widow told him to cut it out and stick to her. He said no. She said yes. Maybe Butman cut her up and someone knew about it—and shot him up. How's that?"

I yawned. "It's great," I told him, "but it isn't what happened."

Phil Dobe grinned. "All right," he said cheerfully. "What did happen?"

I shook my head. "What happened up in Duquesne I don't know. But look here—over in New York Cherulli handles beer and whisky. He has to pass along some coin and it gets lost. He gets killed. The woman he's playing along with gets killed. And a couple of cheap crooks just out of the Big House get killed. And—"

"And you call a dick in and watch him kill one of those cheap crooks," the city editor cut in. "I read the papers, even if they don't write 'em in New York the way we do out here."

I nodded. "That cheap crook shot out Dot Ellis," I reminded him. "He confessed. Said the big guys had him both ways. I did that two-year stretch for Dot, and I still like some of the things she used to do. I owed her something."

Dobe sang a few bars of the *Lohengrin* "Wedding March" and swore.

"Sure," he agreed. "Go on with the story, Mal."

"Donelly shot Garren in self-defense," I said. "I came out here, and right away there's a double murder in Duquesne. Funny."

"Depends on your sense of humor," Phil observed. "You did come out here—and there was a double murder. But then, there was a triple murder in Duquesne last week. And a single one the week before. There's so many up there that they don't count."

"I've got a hunch these two did count," I told him.

"What are you trying to do, Mal?" he asked suddenly, letting his dark eyes slit on mine. "You're fairly young, passably good-looking—and you can move your arms and legs. Why mix in with a bunch of killers?"

I shook my head. "Dot Ellis wasn't any killer," I told him. "Wirt Donner never squeezed a rod. Maybe Garren figured he'd rather let that dick I called in get him than take the juice. I had him cold. I don't think Angel Cherulli ever killed. They weren't killers, Phil—the big ones are the killers, the ones that breed the stuff."

He stared at me. "What stuff?" he muttered.

I looked foolish. "Crime," I replied.

"God!" he muttered. "You *have* gone reformer!"

I grinned. "There never was two hundred grand in this deal, Phil," I told him. "Maybe a hundred, but I don't think so. Maybe fifty—that's more like it. Or maybe something else."

Dobe swore softly. "You certainly are hot," he muttered. "How come you hook up Butman and the Widow with the New York killings?"

That was one I didn't want to answer, so I stalled off. I told him that I'd heard Cherulli and Butman were acquainted, and that that was why I'd come out. I didn't mention Virgie Beers or the Donner woman. Dobe sat back and smiled. When I got through he stood up.

"Mal—" he said slowly—"I've got a hunch. You always did have a yen for crime detection. You got heroic and did a stretch for that tart of yours. You met a lot of crooks up the river, and maybe you learned some things. I think you're working for somebody. You're a private dick."

I tried to look serious. At the moment I couldn't figure any harm in Phil's guessing that way.

"I'm tired and I'm going to bed," I told him. "Where's my bag?"

He grinned, swore, called to the copyboy. He told him to get my bag. Then he swore directly at me. "I wanted to see you before you got the bag," he stated. "So I had Zep stick it in a safe place. Lay off imitating my reporters—and instead of going to bed come along with me and down a few."

I shook my head. "Maybe tomorrow night," I said. "I've only been out of the Big House a few days and my muscles act that way."

Phil Dobe frowned. The copyboy came along with the bag, and Dobe pointed to me.

"Give it to Handsome," he ordered. "Did it leak?"

The copyboy grinned and handed me the bag. Dobe and I went down the steps together. On the street he hailed a cab.

"Give me a break, Mal," he urged. "Remember, I'm not raising hell about what you did tonight. If you know anything—"

He broke off, got inside the cab. I waved at him, went up to the café, and had coffee and a sandwich. There was a phone booth inside the place and I called up the Gurley House. A weary-sounding voice answered my first question by telling me that a Mrs. Howard Evans was registered there. I told him to connect me with the room. There was a little wait and then I heard Virgie Beers's voice.

"This is hubby," I told her. "Was the trip to the city a nice one?"

She said that it was all right, and I asked her if she was alone. She said that Mrs. McClellan was with her, and I guessed that she meant the Donner woman. I told her I'd be over in the morning around ten, and she said she'd be glad to see me. I hung up, walked five blocks to the Seventh Avenue Hotel, got a room with a bath. After a shower I climbed into bed, had two drinks, and tried to do some expert thinking. It came down to a lot of guessing, but it helped a little.

I finally got the facts lined up—the ones I figured were straight. Angel Cherulli, in New York, had been careless with some coin. Some big coin, but not so big as I'd heard. Babe Mullens, the Harlem blues singer he'd been playing with, had claimed two hundred grand was missing. I figured she was bluffing. Virgie Beers said one hundred grand. I didn't like that so much either. It sounded like too much money. Dot Ellis, who had been in soft with Angel until he had fallen for the Mullens brown baby, had come up to see me on my way out of the Big House. Ben Garren, a crook not too long out of Sing Sing, had murdered her. I figured he'd tried to frame me, but he hadn't. Herb Steiner, a cheap fence, had known enough about the Ellis kill to say funny things about it, on the train down from the prison town. I'd had a meet date with Wirt Donner, but he'd been murdered as I'd gone up the steps of the New York boardinghouse. Virgie Beers had been in that house. I'd trapped Garren for the Ellis kill, and Donelly had shot him down as he'd reached for his gun.

That was easy enough. But Steiner had come over and searched my bag for something not there. Virgie Beers had cleared out, and the boardinghouse landlady had sold me her Duquesne address. Cherulli had been gunned a few hours before Dot had got the works. The coke-eater the bulls had picked up for the murder of Wirt Donner had been framed, and he'd passed out in the police station. Virgie swore she didn't know who got Wirt, and I believed her.

I smoked three pills and tried to figure who carved up the Widow, up in Duquesne, and why Butman had been given the works after he'd taken me out in the country for a walk back. It was no good—I couldn't figure it. But I had a hunch that maybe Virgie Beers could. She'd lived in the next house. And the red-haired woman who lived with her was Wirt's sister. That was a kick—and a help.

The things I wanted to know were why Ben Garren finished Dot, why Dot came up to see me out of the Big House, who murdered Wirt Donner, the Widow, and Butman—and why Herb Steiner had gone through my bag. It added up to a lot of things that I wanted to know. I figured Virgie Beers knew some of the answers, and Herb Steiner knew some. I decided that Virgie would be easier to get along with than Steiner.

I fell asleep while I was trying to figure why I should think that.

2

It was cold the next morning—cold and murky. Smoke hung over the city, and everybody looked dirty. I had breakfast in a restaurant where the waiters kept out of my way and let me read the morning paper. It was the *Post-Dispatch*. Chief Butman made the first page. It was "alleged" that he'd been having an affair with the Widow, a "notorious Duquesne character." The paper seemed to feel that Butman might have been responsible for the Widow's carving up, but they weren't quite sure who'd filled him with lead. The Duquesne police, aided by county officers, had the usual clues. So far that was all they had.

It was nine thirty when I walked down toward the Gurley House. I took my time, and kept my eyes open. The city had changed a lot since I'd moved eastward. But it was just as dirty as ever.

The hotel was a good second-class establishment, located on a noisy street about four squares from the spot where Pittsburgh's two rivers hooked up and became one. It was old, and the desk clerk was old. The lobby needed paint. The place was run by the daughter of the wife of the original owner, and she was a religious woman. The hotel looked that way. It had a musty sort of dignity.

I told the clerk that I was Howard Evans, and that my wife was among those who were guests. He told me she was in room 303, and designated a room phone. I got the room.

"This is hubby," I told Virgie. "How are you?"

"Sick as hell." Her voice sounded flat and disagreeable. "I had awful dreams."

I told her that was too bad, and said I was coming up. She said all right. The elevator had just left, so I walked. The higher up I got, the worse the hotel looked. Three hundred and three was down toward the end of the hall. The carpet was faded and the place smelled of disinfectant.

Three raps on the door brought the red-haired one. I let her have a shock in a hurry.

"Hello, Miss Donner—you look great this morning."

She didn't look great, but she did look surprised. I stuck my left hand inside my light coat's left pocket and made a pack of cigarettes shape something like the muzzle of a gun. Then I walked in past her.

The room had two beds. One was made up, but Virgie Beers occupied the other. Her face was pale. She tried to smile, and it made her look worse than ever.

"Sorry I'm not up," she said in a flat voice. "I feel like the devil."

I nodded, tossed my hat on the dressing table, hauled

a chair over to the window, and faced it toward the beds and the door. Then I sat down. The Donner woman came in and stood near the foot of Virgie's bed. There were scattered sheets of morning papers on the floor near the bed.

"You had a close go," I stated. "The late Mr. Butman was anxious to see you both."

Virgie Beers did something that looked like a shiver. The red-haired woman smiled coldly. I sat back in the chair and asked a question. "Come through, Virgie— who carved the Widow?"

She sat up and swore at me. The Donner woman frowned. I tried something else. It was a blind guess.

"You're lying to me part of the way, Virgie. Somebody's after something, but it isn't a hundred grand. It isn't fifty grand. It isn't any grand. Maybe it's stones."

I had a smile on my face, and I had to fight to keep it on. Virgie Beers showed fear in her eyes. The redhead sucked in her breath and went into a coughing spell. I whistled softly.

"Well, well," I said cheerfully. "Now what *sort* of stones do you think they are?"

Virgie dropped her head back on the pillow again and muttered something I didn't get. The Donner woman kept on coughing.

"Water's good for that," I told her. "Or maybe you've got something better."

She turned her back on me. I looked at Virgie.

"Better be good," I suggested. "I got you out of a bad mess last night."

"Or maybe you got me into one last night," she said grimly. "I had some dreams last night, as I said before. You didn't figure so good in them, Mal."

I grinned. The "Mal" sounded too good to be worth anything much.

"If you believe in dreams you probably *do* think Cherulli was playing with a hundred grand when he got the works.''

She just frowned. ''Babe Mullens says he was playing with two hundred grand,'' she said.

I nodded. ''There isn't that much money in the world. You just read there is.''

The Donner woman had finished coughing. She faced me and made a speech.

''Lay off Virgie, Mal. She isn't doing anyone dirt. You're just out from behind the iron—and the bulls'll be watching you. Go back to New York and tell 'em what you know.''

I told her to sit down and take some weight off her big feet. I said that I'd do as I wanted to do, and I'd do as I wanted to do the way I wanted to do it.

''Yeah?'' she came back. ''Maybe.''

I didn't like that. But it was a cinch that Virgie had been on the receiving end of some talk. She wasn't so upset as she'd been last night in Duquesne. And she wasn't so friendly. I began to think that the Donner woman figured in things.

''Wirt didn't speak of you much, up the river,'' I told her. ''He did talk about Virgie, here—but not by name. He wasn't mixed up with a mob, before he went up. He didn't have to change his name to Ross. What was he worried about?''

The red-haired one laughed. It was a hard, metallic laugh.

''You don't know, eh?'' she asked.

I shook my head. ''I don't.''

She muttered something that sounded like ''liar'' and went back toward the door. I lifted up the left-hand pocket of my coat and told her to stick inside the room. She turned around and got sore.

''You and Herb!'' she raved. ''You pick on women to go for the dirty end of—''

"Shut up, Red!" Virgie cut in sharply.

I sat back and grinned. "You talk too much," I told her. "You're going to get shoved out, I can see that. And you know about the stones—"

Fear was showing in her eyes. Her body was tense. I'd used the stone gag the second time and I was more sure than ever that it wasn't a blind trail. Virgie spoke up.

"Sit down, Carrie—for God's sake sit down."

The red-haired one sat down on the made-up bed. She kept her eyes on me; they were narrowed and there was a lot of hatred in them.

"Here's a Ripley," I told them both. "Wirt Donner and I were going after the big guns in the mob that was using up a lot of underdog crooks. We were going to use my coin and go after 'em hard. But they got him before I got to him. If you two tell me things—it'll make it easier."

Virgie Beers got rid of something that was almost a sneer.

"Easier for you," she stated.

"And for you," I said.

Carrie Donner laughed harshly. But there wasn't a hysterical note in it.

"That's a Ripley all right," she agreed. "Believe it, Virgie?"

Virgie propped herself up against a pillow and looked worried.

"You know more than you're telling," she told me.

I nodded. "That makes me even with you," I told her. "But look—I could talk a little and the Duquesne bulls would be grabbing you for a conference."

Her eyes got wide. "What for?" she asked.

"For passing the stuff to the Widow," I said.

Her lips parted—her body stiffened up. Carrie Donner swore huskily. Virgie rolled over on her stomach, buried her face in the pillows, and started to cry. It wasn't pleasant to hear, but there wasn't much else to do. I watched Red—she was keeping her eyes narrowed on mine. After a while Virgie stopped crying and Carrie spoke.

"You got 'em?" she asked.

I was getting somewhere, but there was no telling just where. I shook my head.

"Butman got 'em," I told her. "But he didn't keep 'em. If you talk sense we may be able to do something."

Virgie Beers sat up and wiped her face with a scented handkerchief. She looked pretty bad.

"I wish to God I was on a boat going somewhere!" she wished.

I nodded. "So did Dot Ellis, just before she got her dose," I said. "That isn't even original."

There was a little silence and I tried to figure what it was that Carrie Donner had thought I might have, and that I had said Butman had. Stones—I was pretty sure of that. Maybe diamonds, maybe not.

Carrie Donner got up from the bed, came over and stood in front of me. She said that she could talk better if I'd take my left hand out of my coat pocket. Virgie Beers said that I wasn't left-handed, anyway. I got the hand in sight.

"Come clean with us—and we'll play with you," Carrie said. "Maybe you were going straight with Wirt— maybe you weren't."

I smiled at her. "I'm not trying to appear virtuous," I said, "but I didn't do that stretch for being a crook. I did it because I fed a woman too much booze, and she got driving the car I was in carelesslike."

The red-haired one nodded. "She was a crook, even before you fed her the booze," she stated.

I said that it was a possibility, but I hadn't been aware of it. Virgie laughed. Carrie Donner swore.

"The thing is," she said, "she went up to frame you— she had the stuff with her. It didn't work. Ben Garren got her—and the stuff. After that it dropped out of sight.''

I lighted cigarettes for both women, blew out the match, lighted a fresh one for myself. The way things were going there was no use taking any chances.

''Yeah?'' I said. ''Where'd she get the stuff?''

Carrie Donner smiled nastily. ''In case you don't know,'' she said sarcastically, ''I'll give you a big surprise. From Angel. And I suppose you don't know where he got the green ice?''

I inhaled and let that sink in. Carrie was telling me things, but she didn't think that she was. Emeralds— green ice. And she figured that Dot Ellis had got them from Angel Cherulli and had tried to hand them over to me. She figured that Ben Garren had got them, after doing in Dot, and she wanted me to believe that after he'd grabbed them they had dropped out of sight.

''All right, Carrie,'' I said softly. ''I almost believe you. I was in the Big House when the first part of this deal was working out. Where'd Angel get the green ice?''

She looked at Virgie, who nodded her streaked face.

''You're gabbing,'' she said. ''Go the limit.''

The red-haired one frowned. ''I hate to tell humans stuff they already know,'' she said.

I smiled. ''Sometimes it sounds better the second time.''

She sat down near the foot of Virgie's bed. Her eyes were half closed.

''That South American—Malendez. He was lousy with them. Does business in some damn town in Colombia, down there in South America. Porto Colombia, or something like that.''

''Puerto Colombia,'' I corrected, using a lot of accent.

''You're smart as hell!'' She pulled on her cigarette. ''Well, as I said, this Malendez came up with them. Babe Mullens met him, through Angel. He was at Angel's club, drinking. He got sweet on Babe—and told her she could pick out a hunk of green ice. She did. And then Malendez is hauled out of the East River, all busted up from tug propellers. There's a fuss down in South America and the bulls in New York run around in circles. But nothing happens. It never does.''

I got up, knocked some cigarette ashes from my trousers, sat down again.

"I heard about that, up the river," I told her. "All right—Angel's got the emeralds. Why does Dot Ellis come up with them—to plant them on me?"

Virgie Beers swore. "Angel wasn't running the mob he was in. He was just one of the boys. The green ice was worth maybe a hundred grand. The big boys wanted it. Angel had to get rid of it."

I nodded. "He was on the outs with Dot Ellis—and yet he gave the stuff to her."

Carrie nodded. "That was why," she said. "They went for Babe Mullens. They rolled her, up in her flat. She was dry."

Virgie looked at me. "You got 'em, Mal?" she asked. "I just want to know so that I can go somewhere else if you have."

I shook my head. "I haven't got 'em, and I haven't seen 'em," I said quietly and deliberately. "I didn't get in the cab with Dot, up at Ossining. She drove off in a mad. She was sore as hell. I traced Ben Garren, through a cab driver who'd seen him. So he got the green stuff, eh?"

No one answered. I looked at Virgie. She was getting a little nervous as I kept it up.

"What's wrong?" she muttered, and then her voice went up a few octaves. "You don't think *I* got 'em—"

"You went over to see Ben, after Wirt got the dose," I cut in.

Carrie Donner spoke quietly. "Virgie didn't even get her peepers on 'em," she said.

I nodded. "All right. There's no rush. What about the Widow?"

"That was something else," Virgie said. "I swear to God it was."

I got up. "As you girlies speak your pieces," I said, "I'm to understand that Angel and Babe Mullens worked Malendez loose from a flock of green stones. And then, because Angel was a little guy and didn't have the right to be a crook for himself, things got hot. A lot of guys quit breathing. They're still doing it—and the green ice is still out of sight."

Virgie Beers scratched her blond head noisily.

"That's close, Mal," she said.

Carrie Donner knocked ashes from her cigarette on the faded carpet.

"Goddam close," she stated flatly.

I looked at her. "You're wise to a lot of things," I said. "That's a bad spot, Carrie."

The red-haired one shrugged her shoulders.

"They tried to suck Wirt in, and he talked to me," she said. "Jeez—I had to listen, didn't I? That's a woman's job—that and producing brats."

I grinned. "You don't look like a family lady," I said.

She swore. "It's because I'm careful," she replied. "What next?"

I moved toward the door. "Use your own judgment," I advised. "If I were you, I'd stick inside this room for a day or so. And if I were Virgie I'd do the same thing."

Virgie Beers watched me get fingers on the knob of the room door. She spoke in a shaky voice.

"You said Butman got the stones, Mal. You said he didn't keep them."

I smiled. "Did I? You said the Widow's carving up was something different, Virgie. That makes us even—we were both lying."

I went out and closed the door. I heard Virgie Beers swear and Carrie Donner laugh harshly. The laugh bothered me. I commenced to feel that the Donner woman was as dangerous as Virgie, perhaps more dangerous. I

remembered that she'd hooked me up with Herb Steiner— "You pick on women to go for the dirty end."
That was something to think about.

Downstairs I looked at the clerk's shiny, blue serge
suit, got him away from the card register, and handed
him a twenty-dollar bill.

"That's for you," I said. "I'm not a crook, and all I
want is to be treated kindly. This is what I want."

While I was telling him, the desk phone rang and he
told a red-faced bellhop that Room 303 wanted orange
juice and cracked ice. Then he came over near me and
listened some more.

· 9 ·

ROOM 651

Ore dust from the blast furnaces not far from the city had drifted over and stained the curtains of the two windows facing on the court a dirty reddish color. Room 336 wasn't much of a suite, but it had a location I liked. The court was a small one—almost directly opposite was room 303. The shades were up in my room, with the lights off. In the other room the lights were on, and the shade of the one window was down. I couldn't see much, but if there was any particular racket I could probably hear. And if the lights were on, maybe someone was inside.

It was dark, but it had only been dark a half hour or so. I flopped on the bed, smoked a pill, and thought things over. I'd spent an hour talking to a jeweler—about emeralds. I'd spent two hours in the morgue of the *Post-Dispatch,* going through old papers and reading up on the Malendez case.

The Malendez case had been just one of those things. He'd been an exporter of emeralds, a gambler, a great guy with the lady-folk. He'd been unmarried. He'd come up on a trip, from South America, but it was not known that he'd had jewels with him. He'd played the high and low spots in New York. His body had been hooked out of the East River. A few sticks of follow-up and he'd dropped out of the papers. He hadn't been rated as a millionaire, and though the police suspected foul play, there had been no proof.

I closed my eyes, grunted, blew smoke at the ceiling, and tried to figure things.

One thing was pretty certain, Virgie and Carrie Donner were trying to carry me along. They weren't telling me anything they didn't think I knew. They were a couple of feeders—but they picked their food.

Emeralds weren't jewels for crooks, I knew that. They didn't have demand, and that meant they were more difficult to dispose of, among other things. Over on Olive Street I'd learned some other things. The green ice was an "expert's" stone. A lot of humans could tell diamond from glass. A lot of humans couldn't tell emerald from glass. The Germans had a neat trick of working in the imperfections found in the finest grade real article. Fences knew all this and would be careful about handling the rich, green stones. Crooks knew it and wouldn't take a chance.

I lighted a fresh pill from an old one, rolled over on my right side and looked toward the dirty curtains.

Just the same, green ice was a money stone. Compared to a diamond of the same size and perfection of stone and cutting, the emerald was more valuable. A hundred grand was a hundred grand, and Angel Cherulli hadn't had to work hard to grab the load. That was my guess. Not with the Mullens mulatto smoothing things for him.

And there was the principle of the thing. Cherulli had been a little guy, and he'd tried to work a fast one. There had been a sudden stop. And Virgie and her red-haired friend wanted me to believe that the stones had got themselves lost somewhere. I wasn't so sure about that.

The phone bell rang and the clerk told me that Mr.

Jackson wanted to see Mr. Evans. I told him send Mr. Jackson up. I got up, pulled down the shades, turned on the lights, got some ice in two glasses, put the gin near the ice. After a while there was a knock, and I snapped the lock, walked around where I couldn't see the corridor, called: "All right" in a wheezy voice, and watched Mr. Jackson come in.

He shut the door behind him, snapped the lock, looked around the room, and spotted me. He smiled, but he didn't speak. He was middle-aged, with a mild, gentle face. His eyes were blue and sort of twinkling; he had nice teeth and a slightly gray mustache. He was medium in size.

I designated a chair. He went over and used it, placing rather slender hands on the dark cloth of his lightweight coat. He kept his eyes twinkling and on mine.

"Phil Dobe, over at the *Post-Dispatch,* said you might not be busy," I said. "I need a little help. But it has to be very quiet help."

He nodded. His voice was thin but not unpleasant. Two fingers of his right hand kept tapping the cloth of his coat.

"The agency is a small one," he said. "Just Callarson and myself. Callarson's in Detroit, and I'm not busy at the moment. Everything is strictly confidential—and quiet. And expensive."

I nodded. "That's all right. But this isn't a worried husband job. I've been sort of sticking with it for a few days, and there have been some kills. There may be some more."

He kept on smiling. "It will be expensive," he said again. "My life-insurance premiums have always been high."

I offered him a cigarette, which he refused.

"If anything happens along the way—you don't know me," I said. "It's a tailing job—I just want to be kept informed on the movements of one person. The job may only last a day—it may last a week. How much?''

He smiled and said he thought a hundred a day would be about right for a short order. I nodded and handed him two fifties. He folded them very carefully and got them out of sight.

"Who's my party?" he asked.

I described Virgie Beers, giving her name as Mrs. Evans. I gave him the number of the room, told him of the location. I mentioned that Mrs. Evans was sharing her room with a red-haired woman, but I said I didn't care about her, except that I wanted to know if she went out with Mrs. Evans or not. I told him I'd check out of the hotel, page him as Eric Stanley in about a half hour, and tell him where he could report to me every few hours.

He nodded. "I'll be down in the lobby," he said. "But supposing Mrs. Evans goes out?"

"Go with her, and if I don't get you on the page call, call me at the William Penn any time after an hour," I said.

He nodded. I gave him a detailed description again— of both women. I told him that if he felt doubtful I'd point Mrs. Evans out. He said my description was very good—he'd get along well enough. He got up.

"I use the name of Jackson when it might be heard. Nothing else you want to tell me?" he asked.

I shook my head. "Not right now, because all I want is this tailing job. But I repeat—it isn't divorce stuff. Heads up."

He smiled, moved toward the door. I got back near the wall and he went out. I liked the way he had acted. Phil Dobe had said Quirt was one of the best in the business, and I figured maybe he was.

I packed my bag, saw the gin and the glasses, and remembered that I'd forgotten about the drinks. Downing one, I decided that Quirt wouldn't have taken one anyway. His price was pretty stiff, and I had a hunch that either he recognized a face or was doing some guessing. I packed the bag, went downstairs, and checked out. While I was paying up, Carrie Donner came around to the desk. She asked about mail, and there wasn't any. She looked at me, through me, and beyond me. Then she went out the main entrance. She was dressed up, but she looked like the devil anyway.

Quirt was over by the main entrance, looking at the colored section of a paper. Carrie passed within a few feet of him: he held the paper high, but he looked her over. I took my bag, went over to a corner of the lobby, and sat down. After about fifteen minutes Virgie came down. She was dolled up in a green ensemble with a tight-fitting turban. She carried a briefcase in her left hand. She went to the desk, and the clerk looked in the box. He smiled and shook his head and she smiled and turned away. She didn't look around the lobby, but headed right for the street. Quirt was still reading the colored section. She passed within a few feet of him, and he gave her a thirty-second start. Then he went out.

The clerk was looking at me. I smoked a whole pill, grabbed the bag, and went out. There was no sign of Quirt or Virgie. I hailed a cab, was driven to the William Penn Hotel, registered as Howard Evans, sent the bag up to the room, and bought a paper. I told the clerk I was expecting a phone call in a little while and would take it in the lobby. He made a note of that and I picked out a comfortable chair.

I'd been in it about five minutes when Virgie Beers came in. She went directly to the desk. She talked to the clerk. While she was talking she set her briefcase up where he could see it. She signed a register card. When she looked around the lobby I lifted the paper. She got through doing that about the time a bellhop came in with two bags. They looked pretty new. The clerk gave him a key and he headed for an elevator. Virgie followed him.

I whistled the chorus of "That's My Baby Now"—and watched Quirt come in. He was looking toward closing elevator doors. He waited until they closed—then he ran forward. He called out "Mary!" very loudly. A lot of people heard him and looked around. There were two clerks back of the marble desk—they looked toward the elevators. Quirt acted sort of embarrassed, turned away, turned toward the elevators again—then headed for the desk.

The clerks were smiling. One of them spoke to the other. Quirt asked a question and got an answer. He talked a little to the clerk—they were both smiling. Then he went toward the room phone. I could see his lips moving. After a while he hung up, strolled around the lobby, didn't come very near me, went out. Ten minutes later Carrie Donner came in, went directly to the desk, didn't look around at all, got an elevator, and went upstairs. She had no baggage. Five minutes after that Quirt paged me as Mr. Evans.

"This is Jackson talking," he said. "All right to speak up?"

I told him to go ahead and he said that his party had used two cabs, trying to play safe, had bought two bags in a luggage shop, and had come to the William Penn. She was registered as Mrs. D. Walker in room 651. He had seen me in the lobby and had paged me ahead of time.

I told him his work around the elevators and desk had been sweet, asked him to sit around the lobby for a while, gave him my room number, and said I was going to take a nap. I hung up.

I slid open the door of the phone booth, looked past the switchboard girl, and got a glimpse of a back that looked familiar. I stepped back in the phone booth and

jerked the glass door closed. Herb Steiner walked around
and gave the switchboard girl a number. He stood watching the lobby until she told him the number of the booth.
It was around the other side somewhere. He didn't do
much talking. When he went out into the lobby I took
a lot of pains to keep out of sight.

I spotted Quirt coming in—he had called from some
place nearby. Herb Steiner was buying cigarettes; he
moved toward the elevators. I waited until he was on his
way up above, then went over to Quirt. I touched his
arm, went on past and got behind a palm growing in a
green-based pot. He came around, smiling.

"Go up to Six fifty-one and listen in," I told him.
"There should be three voices inside. Two women and
a man. I'll stick right here—let me know what's what."

He nodded and went away. I had a hunch that Virgie
had been doing some planning. Herb was in town, and
he was at the William Penn. So was Virgie, and so was
Carrie Donner. It looked like a sort of gathering of the
clan. Maybe I was wrong—maybe Herb didn't know that
Virgie and Carrie were around. But my guess was in the
other direction.

In about ten minutes Quirt came down and said that
there was some drinking going on in room 651—he had
heard the ice tinkle. He'd heard one woman's voice and
one man's. The man's had sounded a lot like a woman's,
only it hadn't been.

I smiled. Quirt said that it looked as though the people
inside were making themselves comfortable, that it was
his guess there were only two in there—a man and a
woman.

I told him that they might be making themselves comfortable, but that his guess might be a bad one. I figured
there were three inside. He nodded.

"You figure—or you know," he said quickly.

I smiled, told him to keep his eyes on the elevators.
If Mrs. Evans came down he was to go along with her.

I said she'd probably come down alone, but if she didn't, to stick anyway. And if there was a split-up he was to tail her. He nodded.

"Her face seems a little familiar," he said. "Maybe she's had it used in the papers."

I looked puzzled and told him I didn't follow society doings. He just nodded and smiled. I said I was going up to my room and wash, and he said that the last time I had been going up for a nap.

He was thinking things out, and I didn't like that so much.

"The hundred a day covers just this and that," I reminded. "You don't have to mastermind all over the place for it."

He looked hurt. But he just nodded his head. I went up to the lobby floor, took an elevator to the sixth. Six fifty-one wasn't far from the elevators. I went past the room twice and heard muffled voices the second time. My room was on the fourth floor. I called room service from there, said the phone in 651 didn't seem to be working, said the occupant didn't want it fixed right away, but did want two bottles of Cliquot Club in a hurry. Then I went up and walked past 651 a few more times. A waiter came up with the Cliquot, knocked on the door.

I was ten feet away when Virgie asked who was outside. The waiter told her. She opened the door, said no one had ordered ginger ale, and it must have been a mistake. Someone inside said something I didn't get—and Virgie told the waiter to come in with the stuff. I was close to the door; when he stepped in I stepped in behind him.

Virgie almost clipped me with the door, but I got inside. She let out a little gasp and said: "Ourney!" in a husky voice.

I went right on past her, behind the waiter. Carrie Donner was sitting up on one of the two beds. She stared at me and swore. Herb Steiner was in a chair—his face twisted around; he tried a smile, started to speak, stopped. The waiter set down the tray and the ginger ale and looked at me.

"Hello, Herb!" I said cheerfully. "Hello, Red. Just happened along as the fizzy stuff was being served. How was everything on the Coast when you left?"

I gave the waiter two dollars and said it was my treat. He went out and I got over near a wall and watched Virgie snap the lock on the inside of the door and walk back toward me.

"Tailing, eh?" she snapped. "Why in hell can't you lay off?"

I looked at Herb. His face was pretty white. He looked less like a girl than he had that day on the train. His lips had cruel lines. Both hands were in sight, and both were empty.

"Just an accident," I told Virgie. "Saw Herb come in, and figured I'd better come up and give him something I owe him."

His lips twitched. His rat-like eyes got small. Carrie Donner swore. She was wearing her pet negligee.

"You're a damned liar," she said calmly and nastily. "You tailed us."

I nodded. "All right, put it that way," I said. "I never argue over details. If I'd thought you were going to make a break for it I'd have talked differently, down at the other place."

Virgie went over and stood beside the chair in which Herb Steiner was seated. She had a sullen expression in her eyes. Herb never took his eyes off mine.

I put my right hand out of sight, pulled over an uncomfortable chair with my left, sat down. My back was to the wall—I faced the three of them. I was nearest the door.

"A hundred thousand—four ways," I breathed softly. "That's travel money, eh?"

Virgie sucked in some air and said: "What in hell are you talking about, Mal? It don't make sense."

I looked at Herb Steiner. "You dirty little rat," I said. "Coming with the stuff to my room—over in New York. Trying to plant it on me."

He stared at me, his body moving a little. I watched his right hand.

"Keep your fingers still!" I warned. "You've got pretty hands—I like to look at them."

He spoke in his woman's voice. "I don't know what you're getting at, Ourney. Jeez—I'm telling you straight—"

"He's bluffing." Carrie Donner cut in on him. "He's looking for an excuse—"

There was fear in Virgie's eyes. She spoke in a shaky voice, breaking in on the redhead.

"Herb's all right, Mal—I'm telling you—"

I nodded. "You're telling me that right now," I said. "But it was different this morning."

Steiner looked at me. He looked at Virgie Beers. His eyes were narrowed and his woman lips were pressed tightly together. He was beginning to breathe a little heavily.

Carrie said slowly: "That's a lie, Herb—he's trying to get you thinking things."

I nodded. "Bright girl." I got up and went over close to Steiner. "Sit still—and keep your hands still," I warned. "Who got word to you, Virgie or Red?"

His long fingers were twisting. He parted his lips in a smile that was forced and unreal.

"Better be careful, Ourney," he muttered in his thin whisper. "You know I never tried to plant anything on you."

I got both hands on his throat and jerked him out of the chair. He started to twist. Virgie cried out, and I turned my head.

"Shut up, you damn fool!" I snapped at her. "You'll have the house dick up here—and then where'll you be?"

Steiner was pleading with me in a strained, jerking voice.

"Listen, Ourney—for God's sake—listen—I didn't frame you—"

I used my arms and shook him. I tightened up the grip on his throat. He squirmed around and started to kick. It didn't take me more than about five seconds to shake the kick out of him. Then I shoved him into the chair and looked at Virgie. She was smiling at me.

"Give it to him, Carrie!" she said almost pleasantly.

I didn't look at Carrie. Instead I let my knees buckle, hunched my head forward—dropped. I went down directly in front of the choking Steiner—and he took the slug. The gun in Carrie's grip pop-coughed; it didn't crash. Steiner screamed. It was a shrill, high-pitched scream.

I rolled for the foot of the bed—and the second bullet dug into wood, ricocheted off, and slapped into the wall. I got an arm up and grabbed her by the right ankle—she was crouched on the bed. I jerked—and her third bullet went over my head and made a lot of noise somewhere across the room. Then she lost balance, went over the left side of the bed.

I reached her as she was trying to raise the gun for another try. Her fall had stunned her—I grabbed her right wrist, shook it. She let go of the gun, and I kicked it under the bed. It was a real weapon.

I straightened up and turned around. Virgie Beers was leaning up against the wall, still smiling. But there wasn't anything funny in her smile. And there wasn't anything funny in her right hand. It was a Colt—and she held it low, the muzzle pointed toward my waistline.

"You dirty double-crosser," she muttered. "You've got it coming!"

I didn't feel much like rushing her. Carrie had been

on a tricky-surfaced bed, and she'd missed her first shot. But Virgie had both feet on the floor—she was ten feet away from me, and she was pretty calm.

"You damn fool," I said again. "When they get inside this place—"

She laughed nastily. Her eyes went beyond me in a swift glance.

"Get up, Carrie," she said. "Find that rod and wipe it clean. Come around and look at Herb. See where you bit into him. For Christ's sake don't panic—and give them the Ritzy stuff if they bang on the door. Make it fast."

I smiled at Virgie. "You're good," I said simply. "You're damned good."

She showed her teeth in a smile I didn't like. But she didn't speak. She kept her eyes on mine, and her gun hand was steady. Carrie Donner, breathing heavily, climbed over a bed and got nearer Steiner. He was slumped low in the chair. He looked bad.

Carrie started to sob, and Virgie swore at her. I tried a grin.

"Sure as hell," I said, "you shot that fence out of things."

Virgie's smile went away. She moved her gun a little. It looked something like a Lüger, but it wasn't. It had a long barrel.

"You shut up," she said. "*I* can use a rod!"

Carrie was bending over Steiner. She straightened, turned a white face toward Virgie.

"He's—alive," she said. "There's heartbeats—"

Virgie nodded. "Get over near the door and sing rotten the way you do," she said. "Talk every once in a while—as though you were talking to me."

Carrie Donner moved toward the door. She started to sing. Her first few notes were shaky, broken. Then it got better. She was trying hard. She stopped, and called out in a voice that was almost funny.

"—and I came close to buyin' the chapeau down at Madame Larue's—"

Virgie laughed. It was pretty good. I thought I heard footfalls out in the corridor.

"That hat was no bargain, dearie," she called back.

Carrie started to sing again. Virgie looked at me. She pointed to Herb Steiner, pointed to me, pointed toward the closet.

I took the hint, walked over, and picked him up out of the chair. His vest material was ripped, not far above the belt. He was breathing, but not very heavily. His eyes were closed. There were a lot of finger marks on his throat. I got him into the closet and shut the door. Carrie broke off her singing again.

"I'm going out to see Marie tomorrow," she announced. "They've got a new kid out there."

Virgie laughed again. She pointed toward the chair from which I'd lifted Steiner. I went over and sat down.

"It's about time," she stated. "They haven't had one for over a year."

Carrie cut the singing and hummed. She moved back from the door. She went into the bathroom and ran the water, turned it off, started it again.

I tried to keep any expression of admiration out of my eyes, but I had a hunch it showed. The girls were crooks. Maybe they were killers. They had a lot of rotten tricks. But they had guts.

Virgie Beers whistled. She whistled tunelessly, and every few seconds Carrie cut in with a question or went into the bathroom and ran the water. From the corridor it must have sounded all very homey. And if no one had been occupying the rooms on either side of 651 it looked as though the rod hadn't made much of a racket.

I sat in the chair and tried to figure things out. But my brain wouldn't do that—not with Virgie sticking close with her rod. After a few minutes I spoke in a low voice.

"He's got it in the stomach. If you don't get a doc—he'll be gone."

Virgie nodded. "The fingerprints on his neck will keep," she said. "And maybe you'll be around."

"I was trying to get you a break, Virgie," I said. "I tailed him up here—to see how things were going."

She smiled. The water running in the bathroom covered up our words. Once or twice I thought I heard Carrie Donner sobbing. She was in the bathroom. Virgie smiled with narrowed eyes.

"You saw," she said. "You tried to frame us, Mal—you tried to frame Carrie and me."

I widened my eyes. "Ease off with the rod," I suggested. "It might go off."

She didn't ease off with the rod. She narrowed her eyes a little more and swore softly but nastily.

"You tried to frame us, Mal," she said again.

I groaned. "Didn't I stand you a getaway from the house next to the Widow's?" I muttered. "I got you clear of Butman, didn't I?"

She smiled with her lips. "So you could frame us later," she said. "Or maybe so you could get Butman."

I started to get up from the chair. But Virgie said no sharply and shifted the angle of the rod's muzzle. I sat back and argued. Carrie was still in the bathroom, and the water was still running. No one was bothering us from outside.

"You know damned well I didn't get Butman," I said. "And how did I try to frame you?"

She laughed throatily. "You want to know," she mocked. "You can't guess. Well, maybe you tried to give Steiner the idea we had the green stuff."

I stared at her. "Me—give Steiner the idea—"

I broke off and chuckled. Virgie did the same thing, imitating me. It was a cold imitation. Her features looked sharper than ever—the light in the room didn't help her face any. But her eyes didn't look too dopey.

"Who you working for, Mal?" she asked suddenly. "Come through—and maybe you'll get walking outside again. If you don't come through—well, it's just too bad."

I smiled. Carrie Donner came out and leaned up against the closet door. She looked sick. Down in the street a truck backfired, and she jerked her arms up, bared her teeth. She'd been crying; her eyes were red.

"You talked as if we were going to split a hundred grand," Virgie said slowly. "What was that idea?"

"I was bluffing Herb," I said.

She nodded, but she didn't smile. Without turning her head she called to Carrie.

"We've got Ourney right," she said when the redhead reached her side. "You were nervous on the trigger—but he was a rat, anyway. We can give this baby the same dose—and ten to one we'll get clear—"

"The odds are too high," I cut in, but she didn't pay any attention to my words. Her eyes were on mine; she talked in a low voice to the red-haired one.

"—or we can let him finger the rod—and fix it so that we go out, he stays—and the bulls come in—"

"That'll be tougher," I said.

"—or we can call a number and get Jake to come over. Maybe he can patch Herb up. He's quiet."

I nodded. "You've got to do that in a hurry," I reminded. "Steiner's not getting much of a break, jammed in that closet."

Carrie swore at me. She looked toward the closet, spoke to Virgie.

"If you hadn't of yelled at me to let Ourney have the dose—"

"Shut up," Virgie said in a low, sharp tone. "Keep your voice low."

Her eyes looked squarely into mine. They were almost bright.

"Or you can come across with the green ice, Mal—and walk out that door," she said softly.

I chuckled. "If I admitted I had the stuff it would only be a bedtime story," I said. "Why kid me—when you three were in here for the split?"

She looked at the rod she held—then at me again.

"Come across, Mal!" she said grimly. "You tailed us here—Carrie and me. You didn't expect to see Steiner."

"All right," I said. "If I've got the stuff and I didn't expect to see Steiner—why did I tail you here?"

"Maybe you wanted to spread it out a little. Maybe we might be quieter and take a trip."

I shook my head. "You haven't got anything on me, Virgie," I told her. "I haven't got the stones—and you know it. You're covering up."

She laughed harshly.

Carrie Donner was standing a few feet off and glaring at me. She said: "You did the Dot Ellis job."

I looked at the gun that Virgie was holding, thought about Quirt, down in the lobby, thought about Carrie's coming too close to finishing me, and gave her the works.

"*You* gave Wirt Donner a stomach dose—and you probably did for Herb."

She looked as though she were going to jump at me, but Virgie shot words at her and kept her off. Then the blonde looked at me.

"It wasn't so long ago that you told me *I'd* done for Wirt," she said.

I nodded. "I was kidding."

She said that I was like hell, and that I was tricky as hell, and that it was a hell of a note when two women had to be pulled in for a lot of dirty jobs done by males. She said that she could put me out of things easily enough, and that she felt like doing it.

She was getting a little worked up, and that didn't seem so good. I told her that it wouldn't be so funny if

Steiner went out in the closet. I suggested that the gab
be called off, and that I'd walk out and try again sometime. She laughed that off.

Carrie Donner was getting nervous. She swung on me.

"You goddam reformer!" she accused. "After the big
boys, eh? Why in hell don't you start in with yourself?
You think—"

Virgie told her to shut up, and she said she wouldn't.
Virgie walked over a step or so and slapped her in the
face. I got up from the chair, huddled forward a little,
and jumped for the blonde. Carrie let out a yell—and
Virgie twisted to one side. My right hand got a grip on
her gun arm—I swung her in close to me.

She was mouthing nasty words, and fighting. I got my
left hand against the rod's metal—and saw Virgie's head
twist, her eyes look beyond me. I jerked my own head.

It saved me from most of the blow. But the ginger-
ale bottle was heavy—and Carrie was a good hater. It
caught me over the right ear. Everything got numb and
dark. I let go of Virgie and slipped to my knees. Things
started to buzz. And then I stopped seeing darkness, and
there was no more buzzing. There wasn't much of anything.

· 10 ·

NORTH SIDE

I came out of it slowly. My mouth felt dry and the right side of my head ached. I was lying on my face, and after a few minutes I pulled myself to my knees. I crawled over to the chair I'd been sitting in most of the time, sprawled into it, and looked around. My eyes weren't working so well, but it didn't take me long to see that Virgie and the red-haired one had departed.

The place looked pretty neat. On the floor near one of the beds lay a rod. It was the one Carrie had used in trying to get me. I stood up, tried to walk steadily, and got the rod. There were footfalls in the corridor. I went into the bathroom, used a towel on the gun. It was a pretty sure thing that Virgie had got my fingers on the grip.

When I came out there were no more footfalls. And there was no telling how long I'd been unconscious. I wrapped the gun in a towel, opened a window, set the towel on a narrow ledge that extended beyond the range of eyes inside the room. When I closed the window I sat down on the bed and tried to get over the dizziness. Then I went back in the bathroom, looked at my head.

There was a small cut—and a fair-sized lump over the right ear. I wiped the blood off, went back into the room, got my overcoat buttoned.

My head was pretty clear—I thought about Herb Steiner, went over, and opened the closet door. He was hunched up—his eyes were opened and his head twisted toward me. He muttered something very weakly. I kneeled down beside him.

"I'll go down, outside—I'll call the hotel and have someone find you. Keep your mouth shut. You'll get better just as quickly that way."

His eyes looked pretty bad, but it seemed to me he thought the idea was all right. I spent a minute or so wiping off things I might have touched. Up in the Big House I'd been fingerprinted, and I had to be careful.

I left the closet door open and went out, making sure no one was in the corridor. I couldn't quite figure why Virgie and Carrie hadn't sent someone up in a hurry— unless it was because they were making sure of a getaway first. I walked down to my room, fooled around fixing my hat so it covered the cut on my head. A hurried drink helped. I felt sort of sorry for Herb Steiner, but other things counted, too.

An elevator dropped me to the lobby level; I went out a side entrance, crossed to a cigar store, got a booth, called the hotel, and asked for the manager's office.

A woman's voice answered. I acted excited, pitched my voice a few octaves higher than normal, and said there was a dying man in room 651. I told her it was no joke, and to get someone up there in a hurry. Then I hung up, bought a pack of cigarettes, crossed the street, and came in the main entrance.

There was no sign of Quirt. I went to the desk, told the room switchboard girl that I'd be in the lobby and that I was expecting a call. I felt pretty bad. My head ached and my whole body felt weak. I picked out an overstuffed chair—and parked in it. A page boy came around shouting for a Mr. Einstein, and I had him bring me a paper. It hurt my eyes to look at the print, but it was a screen for my face, if I needed one.

In about ten minutes I heard a siren wail. It got closer to the hotel—then stopped wailing. My chair didn't face the elevators, and I didn't figure they'd carry Herb out through the lobby anyway. About ten more minutes passed, and then the siren started to wail again. It grew more distant and finally an orchestra, playing dinner music somewhere beyond the lobby, drowned it out.

"Nice, clean sheets for Herb!" I murmured. "Red gets the credit line."

It might have been myself they were sirening away, that was a cinch. I couldn't figure it. My head wasn't working well enough. I felt sick. But it was my hunch that either Virgie or Red—or Herb—knew something about the green stones. I hadn't seen any stones, but I believed they existed. Little crooks were invariably stupid—and if emeralds were not a crook jewel—and hard to handle—it was easy enough to believe that the small boys and girls would grab emeralds.

Virgie and the Donner woman had left room 651 together. Quirt had been in the lobby. He'd tailed them, of course. If he could stick, it was fairly likely that I should get another chance. I didn't feel like taking one—but there wasn't much of an out showing. Bed would have suited me better—a lot better.

I read some of the large print in the evening paper. It wasn't a *Post-Dispatch*—it was yellower. The mistress of a steel official had, about five hours ago, found that the steel man was getting fed up with her and planning to transfer his affections. She had walked into his office, all drugged up, and shot him twice. Her aim had been rotten, so far as he had been concerned. But she'd done a nice job on herself. She was dead, and the steel man was looking for alibis. The yellow sheet was laughing them off—and the story had sent the Butman and Widow kills off page one. I found a column on Butman on page three. The police were still looking for clues. The Widow rated a stick or so. The police were looking for a Pole who had been sweet on her six months ago.

I leaned back and closed my eyes. It felt better. It was my idea that maybe I was coming closer to things, but that I was getting kicked around too much.

Herb Steiner had slugged me down. Carrie Donner had done the same trick, only she'd used a ginger-ale bottle. It had hurt more. Virgie had held a gun on me and had come pretty close to talking herself into using it. And Carrie had squeezed lead that had been absorbed by Steiner.

I swore. There was the faint clatter of silver from the direction of the dining room, up behind the balcony that three-sided the lobby. It was seven-fifteen by my wristwatch—and the glass was cracked. That had happened up in room 651. I didn't feel hungry.

At seven-thirty-five the page boy came around and called for a Mr. Evans. I gave him a dime, followed him to a booth, and listened to Quirt asking me if I was Mr. Evans. I said I was and he said he was Mr. Jackson.

"I'm across the bridge—on the North Side," he said. "My party is drinking soup in a café called Lonnie's. She's got a red-haired friend with her, and Red is either coked up or scared to death. They used a cab and a street car getting here, and I can see the café entrance from where I am. They've got luggage—the two new bags and an old one. The cab's waiting outside—and so's mine."

"Not bad," I told Quirt. "Stick along, and if they hole in anywhere that looks permanent, give me a buzz. It's more important than it was an hour ago—so don't lose the blonde. If they split, stick with her. I'll be in my room. Call me there, but don't talk as openly as you are now. They've had an accident at the hotel."

A little curiosity crept into his voice.

"Anything serious?"

"Not for you or me," I told him. "A guy was shot with a gun."

"One of the unloaded ones?" Quirt asked.

I told him the police weren't sure about that yet. He said he'd better be getting closer to the café because it was near a corner and there might be a side entrance. He couldn't see the cab from the phone booth. I wished him luck and hung up. Up in my room I ordered soup and some light food. I kept the right side of my head away from the waiter. After I'd eaten I lay down and tried to think. It hurt so much that I quit. Sleeping was easier.

2

The phone bell woke me up and sent a lot of nasty vibrations through my aching head. I switched a light on, looked at my watch. It was ten thirty. I picked up the receiver and told Quirt that Mr. Evans was talking. He said that he was over at Mary's place and that Joe was glad to know I was in town and did I want to play some golf tomorrow. I told him I'd be too busy with the Charlie Cleaver deal, and he said that Mrs. Somers had been in and was anxious for me to look at the Matisse she'd picked up. I told him that was fine. He said that his Aunt Lizzie was coming on in a few days, and he hoped I'd stay over long enough to meet her. I said I hoped so.

I was getting sort of bored and asked him if he couldn't tell me something that was news, and he said that the way things were breaking I'd have to stall them off on the pipe deal. He said a certain party was pressing him. I got the idea that Virgie or the Donner woman was in close.

He used a lot of words and names, and every once in a while he'd stop and I'd use a lot of words and names.

It was getting monotonous. And then he cut it out and talked sense.

"They didn't split," he said. "The place is called the Harris House. It's a cheap hotel about three blocks from the North Side end of the Third Street bridge. They finished feeding, took the cab to a picture show. Came out after getting a lot of talk-and-sound effects, walked with the bags to the Harris House. They've got a room I can spot from outside, but I didn't go in. Wanted to save my face—don't think they've eyed it yet, and the lobby is small. I'm talking from a tobacco shop, and Red just came in for some pills. She's gone back."

I told him to stick around and to call me from another place in fifteen minutes. I needed that much time to think. We both hung up. I went over and opened the window all the way. It was pretty chilly, and the air helped. There wasn't any way to figure it—so I decided to go over to the North Side and look over the Harris House. I dressed slowly, waiting for Quirt's next call. One thing was evident—Virgie was sticking in town. My idea of the reason was that it had something to do with green ice.

3

The Harris House was a three-story, dirty brick building on a street a block from a cheap-stored main street. The cold wind that swept in from the river didn't bring very pleasant odors along with it. I walked around past the side entrance and looked at the lights in a few of the windows. They didn't tell me anything. Then I walked around past the main entrance. Across the street I saw Quirt. I went a block toward the river, turned toward the main street. Quirt came along slowly, and when I stopped to light a cigarette he came up.

"They're still inside," he said, smiling at me. "What's the matter with your head?"

I smiled back at him. "Careless of me. I walked into a door."

He grinned. "I'd like to see it done—that way. You must have been walking sideways."

He had the gentle smile playing around his lips. I nodded. We turned and went back to the corner, from which place we could see one entrance of the hotel.

"You had both entrances spotted?" I asked.

He nodded. "I kept moving around," he said. "The blonde's face is familiar."

That was the second time he'd mentioned that face. I came through.

"Her name's Virginia Beers—she's from New York. She might be mixed up in the Cherulli murder. She might be mixed up in the Wirt Donner kill. She might be mixed up in the carving of the Widow in Duquesne, and in Butman's gunning out. There are other mights, but perhaps that helps."

He whistled softly. "Thanks," he said. "Must have seen her face in the papers."

I didn't think much of that. *I* hadn't seen Virgie's face in the papers. The newshounds hadn't figured her that important. There was something about Quirt that I didn't like. But I couldn't figure what.

We went around the corner, crossed a narrow street, got in the shadow of a building that had no windows on the side street. Quirt pointed out a window on the top floor, at the rear. A shade was down—there were lights on.

"That was dark when they came in—I walked around here and had a look. Then I went around front. When I came back it was lighted."

I grunted. "Maybe someone got up and turned on the lights," I said.

He nodded. "Maybe," he said. "But the two ladies had just about enough time to get up there. And no other lights flashed on."

That was better. I stood beside Quirt and looked up at the room. I decided that the best thing would be to close in on Virgie again, but with a little help.

"Got a gun?" I asked Quirt.

He nodded. "I live in a bad section," he replied. "Carry it for protection."

"Sure," I returned. "We'll go in and take a room. Then we'll make a call. I'll do the calling, and you just come along with your smile—and the gun."

He didn't say anything. I gave him a break.

"I'll donate another hundred—for your company on the call," I said.

He didn't speak, and I led the way toward the entrance of the Harris House. I almost got a smile from the thought that this would be the fourth hotel I'd hit since dawn. Seventh Avenue, Gurley House, William Penn—and now the Harris House. But it wasn't too funny.

We were ten feet from the entrance when two cars came down the street, moving fast. There was a vacant store on the left of the hotel—the entrance was dark. I shoved Quirt back in the shadow, stepped back myself. The two cars pulled up in front of the hotel entrance. There was no squeal of brakes. Men got out of each car, and they got out in a hurry. But the drivers stuck. The cars were black in color and sedans.

I got my lips close to Quirt's left ear.

"We're going inside—stick close."

He nodded. I stepped out, made a quick turn, went through the hotel door. Things had happened fast inside. A gray-haired clerk was lying behind the desk—red staining his hair. From up above there was the sound of footfalls on thinly carpeted steps.

Quirt swore softly. I headed for the stairs, ten feet beyond the small lobby desk. The carloads of men were going to do something, and they were going to do it fast. They were working crudely, but it wasn't because they didn't know better.

I was halfway up the first flight of steps when the door crashed. It made a lot of racket—as if men had put their weight against it. There was a high-pitched scream. Then the shooting started. There was a lot of it, but it only lasted about five seconds. It stopped.

A hoarse voice sounded from another flight or so up. It got out just one word. "Outside!"

We reached a landing—Quirt pulled me toward a dim, red light along the hall. There were men pounding down the steps above. Quirt put his weight against a door. We got out on a narrow fire escape, shoved the door closed. The escape was on an alley. The pounding of feet grew louder. A door slammed, below. I pulled open the fire escape door, headed for the stairs. Quirt was behind me. We went up two flights—light streaked into the dingy corridor from a room whose door was open. The location was right. It was the room Quirt had pointed out.

I ran for the room, with Quirt behind me. He was muttering something about "police"—but that was why I was hurrying. Faintly I heard the sounds of cars picking up speed through the shifts. I reached the room. There was plenty of light inside.

Carrie Donner was lying near the window. I went in.

Quirt came in behind me and muttered: "They got— the redhead."

He was right. There wasn't a doubt. A lot of guys had squeezed lead on the red-haired one, and it didn't look as though any of them had missed. She was through.

I took a quick look around the room. There were three bags. There was no sign of Virgie. There was no bathroom. I spoke to Quirt.

"Go back to the head of the stairs—call out if you hear anyone coming up. On your way take a look and see if that fire escape is right on this floor."

He nodded, went out. I got a handkerchief wrapped around my right hand, opened a closet door. Virgie wasn't inside. There were two or three bugs crawling around.

I closed the door, listened to a police whistle shrill, a block or so away, went over and looked at Carrie. My eyes picked up a glow of color, near her right hand. I picked up the glow. It was a small stone—a rich green in color.

Quirt sang out. "Let's go!" His voice was low, strained.

I took a last look at Carrie. She looked bad. I slipped the stone in my right lower vest pocket, met Quirt at the fire escape door. We went down—dropped into an alley, came out on the side street, walked away from the sound of a police whistle shrilling from in front of the hotel. They'd found the hotel clerk.

We reached the main street and strolled, looking in windows.

Quirt said: "We got there a little late."

I swore softly. "We might have been too soon," I told him. "Mrs. Evans wasn't there."

He smiled with his lips. "Virgie Beers must be a wise kid," he said.

We stopped in front of a pet store and watched some pups sleeping. I thought of the green stone in my vest pocket, of Virgie Beers, and of the fact that the room hadn't had a bath attached. The green stone interested me most. But Virgie came next. Carrie was out—it was too bad, but she ceased to figure when she stopped moving around and lying.

"Where do you suppose Mrs. Evans got to?" Quirt asked.

I passed the cigarettes—we both lighted up.

"Maybe she was taking a bath," I replied.

He nodded. "I thought of that," he said. "Even looked for the bathroom—couldn't spot it. Maybe on the floor below."

I said maybe. He wanted to know what next. It was too tough for me. I told him he might work the North Side station to see what they got out of it. And he might play around the Harris House without getting too close.

I told him to ring me at the William Penn in an hour. He said he might not be able to pick up Mrs. Evans again. He said he could run over to the morgue now and then. She might turn up there.

He smiled his gentle smile. There was something about him I didn't like. But I smiled back at him.

"Use your own judgment, Mr. Jackson," I said. "I'd like to get in touch with Mrs. Evans—quietly."

He nodded, moved along. I stood for a few seconds and watched the pups sleep. A siren made sound, but didn't get very near the lighted street. I put a right-hand finger in my vest pocket and touched the green stone. It felt cold.

· 11 ·

OVAL FACE

It was ten minutes to midnight when I rode up in the ancient elevator and walked over the creaking boards of the *Post-Dispatch* editorial rooms. Phil Dobe was standing up behind his desk—he glared at me as I came along. When I got up close enough he used words. "You're just two jumps ahead of the bulls, Mal. What'd you do—go out the back way?"

I looked puzzled. There were a couple of good cigars lying beside a blue pencil—I took one of them, bit off an end, lighted up. Dobe swore at me.

"What you holding out on me for?" he demanded. "Haven't I covered you up?"

I grinned. "What do you mean—holding out? I've been sleeping a lot."

He swore again. "Not so much—you haven't," he muttered. "But you know someone who's sleeping right now."

I told him his cigars were stronger than the *Post-Dispatch* circulation, said that his taste in neckties was improving, and asked him what had happened to the tall blonde he used to take out after "thirty"—and watch her drink coffee from the saucer.

He suggested that I was an illegitimate child, doing it in two words. He sat down and glared up at me.

"A woman named Carrie Donner got the works, over in a cheap hotel on the North Side. She's been identified. A red-haired jane. Her brother was bumped off in New York a few days ago. Maybe you heard about that?"

I nodded. "I was there just after he got shot. So he had a sister, eh?"

Phil Dobe groaned. "Stop me if I'm telling you something you don't know," he said sarcastically. "A guy got shot in the belly—at the William Penn, maybe a couple of hours before the Donner woman got her dose. He may live. His name's Eddie Flynn—that's all the doctors would let the bulls find out."

I sat on the desk and looked interested.

"We had an Emma Flynn cooking for us when I was a kid. Maybe he's some relation."

Dobe nodded. "Or maybe he's Herb Steiner," he said grimly.

I pulled on the cigar. The city editor was watching me closely.

"Come through, Mal," he said suddenly. "You may need me, later."

I thought that over and ended up by nodding. I got off the edge of the desk, pulled up a battered chair close to his, sat in it.

"I'll talk a little, Phil," I said. "But you've got to use the stuff I give you the way I want you to use it. It'll still be news. I'll have to have your word for that. Me first—the paper next."

Dobe grunted. "You would," he said dryly. "All right. Tell me what's up."

I shook my head. "If I knew that, I wouldn't tell you. It happens that I don't know. But here's something:

there've been a flock of killings, seemingly related. They started right after I got out of stir—and they're still going. They've taken the play away from me. I had an idea, and Wirt Donner was in on it. We were going to try and get at the few big crooks through the little ones they worked on."

Dobe acted impatient. "I heard about the wet-nursing stuff," he said. "It's no good. Even cheap crooks hate reformers."

I nodded. "They'd protect the ones higher up, I'll agree there—if they could. But a lot of them are stupid."

"The stupid ones die off," Dobe said grimly.

"Or stand the raps," I added. "Anyway, Carrie Donner wasn't my idea of a stupid lady. Some of the clever ones get it, too."

Phil leaned forward and tapped on his desk with the knuckles of his right hand. The noise from the A. P. machines and the clatter of the typewriters drowned out the sound his knuckles made.

"To hell with theory," he said. "Give me something I can feed into the presses."

I shook my head. "I'll give you the story—and some theory," I told him. "But you can't use it until there's a break. When that happens, if you play with me now, I'll give you everything. It'll be a steal. Yes—or no?"

He stuck out his barrel chest and narrowed dark eyes on mine. His face was all twisted up in a frown. I sat back and pulled on the cigar. Dobe swore a couple of times.

"Yes," he said jerkily. "Who got Carrie Donner?"

I laughed at him. "You'd make a good crook. If I knew that and told you—you'd use it for a head. I don't know."

Phil relaxed a little. "What's all the shooting for?" he asked in a changed tone.

I reached in my pocket and put the green stone on the scarred wood of his desk. Light from a green-shaded bulb hit it. It looked nice. The city editor leaned forward and stared at the stone. The color was a rich green—and yet it was transparent. Dobe grunted.

"What is it?" he asked. "It's green."

"No?" I rolled it over with my right forefinger. "You've been studying."

Dobe poked it around. It was cut in oblong fashion, with angular corners.

"Looks like a coffin, something," he muttered. "A nice, green coffin."

I nodded grimly. "It looks like that to a lot of humans," I said.

The city editor stopped poking it. His dark eyes met mine.

"Emerald?" he asked.

I shrugged. "Haven't had time to learn that," I said. "Do it in the morning. You playing with me until I give you the print sign?"

He looked at the stone—then nodded his head.

"Where'd you get it?" he asked.

"Found it lying near one of Carrie Donner's dead hands," I said.

He whistled softly, lighted a cigar that had gone out, whistled again, poked the stone some more. Then he looked at me.

"Well?" he questioned.

The fire alarm started to bang out a call-box number. Out of the corner of my eyes I watched the one rewrite man still on duty thumb a little red book and shake his head.

"Brooker and First," he called across to Dobe. "Nigger town."

Phil told the copyreader to see that Levy didn't try to hop a cab and chase the fire. He said that Levy had a dark girl up around Brooker somewhere. The copyreader said he didn't have her anymore—that he was chasing a jane with a Turk name. Phil said he didn't believe that, and the copyreader said he did because he'd seen the girl, and Levy was training his mustache to look just like hers. Phil thought that was pretty funny. Levy sat before a typewriter, took it all in between noisy yawns. Phil looked at the stone, then at me again.

"Well?" he repeated.

"Babe Mullens and Angel Cherulli are supposed to have worked a guy named Malendez—a South American—loose from a flock of these, Phil. Angel forgot to pass the stuff along to the big guys. They closed in— and he passed the stones to Dot Ellis. Things started to happen."

Dobe whistled again. I picked up the green stone and slipped it into a vest pocket. He watched it disappear, but he seemed to be thinking about other matters.

"Who told you that?" he asked, after a while.

"Carrie Donner," I replied.

"Believe it?"

I swore softly. "Haven't got around to that point yet," I said. "Been too busy."

He nodded. "Who shot Herb Steiner?" he asked. "The bulls recognized him—but they made my police man promise to keep quiet."

I took a chance. "Carrie shot him—but her aim was rotten. She was trying for me. That's out, Phil. If you use it—I'll cover up what comes next."

He grunted. "Hell!" he said softly. "So you were there, too. Just luck?"

I shook my head. "It took a couple of us to get me nearly killed," I said. "I'm using your man Quirt."

He looked at my head, smiled. "Don't kid me, Mal," he said. "I'll tell you another dick who's pretty good. I didn't know until an hour ago that Quirt was up in Canada."

I sat up straight, tried not to look at him. I coughed a few times.

"Just the same," I said slowly, "I've been using a bird who passed himself off as Quirt. He said Callarson was in Detroit."

Phil stared at me. "The hell he did!" he muttered. "Jimmy Rellis was in here—he said Quirt left for Canada yesterday. Went up to join his partner—they're trying to trace some split payroll coin. How'd you get this guy who says he's Quirt?"

"Called the number you gave me—got some girl, asked for Mr. Quirt. Man answered. Told him I was Howard Evans, and that you had said he might be able to help me. He said he'd come over, and I told him where. He came."

The city editor was frowning. "What'd he look like?" he asked.

"Middle-aged—mild smile. Gentle blue eyes. Gray mustache, nice teeth. Medium in size. Thin hands. Thin, quiet voice. Works pretty smoothly."

Phil Dobe smiled grimly. "I'll say he does," he said. "Almost as smoothly as the real gent."

2

We sat in my room at the William Penn. Phil Dobe had a quart of bad red wine—we were gaining on it. It was after one, and there had been no call from Quirt. The city editor sprawled in his chair, a faint smile on his face.

"If he comes—we'll learn things," he said slowly. "When I worked the North Side police beat, there was that guy Gleason. Jeez—but he could take it out of a man. And he didn't use any rubber hose or leave marks."

I shook my head. "You can't get anywhere that way—not in this deal," I said. "The thing for me to do is to stop making mistakes."

Dobe grunted. "Getting to be a damned Pollyanna,"

he said. "That's the thing for us all to stop doing—but we never get around to it. "And then again, there's virtue in making mistakes."

I swore softly. "Not from where I'm sitting, there isn't."

I lighted a fresh cigarette and Phil took another drink of the wine.

"Let's see—there's this old gal of yours—Dot Ellis. There's Wirt Donner, the Widow, Chief Butman—and now Carrie Donner. You think the bulls in New York gave that bird Salmon the final slams. You and some dick got this bird Ben Garren—"

"That was open and shut," I cut in. He murdered Dot. And don't forget Angel Cherulli. They mobbed him out."

Phil Dobe nodded. His dark eyes were half closed.

"I think you're still holding out something, Mal," he muttered. "But even if you are—that's a lot of killing for a flock of stones that won't market for more than fifty grand *if* they're worth a hundred right now."

I was willing to agree on that. Dobe shook his head slowly.

"They try to push you under—and Carrie gets Herb Steiner in the stomach. He's your man, Mal—he knows things. I'll have the boys watch the City Hospital—we don't want him to get well too quickly."

"The bulls'll hold him, even if he gets out of the hospital," I suggested.

Phil wasn't so sure of that. He said it depended on what sort of a greasing job Herb could handle. There wasn't much of a charge against him. The only thing he'd done was to get shot in the stomach.

We sat in silence for a while. Then Phil spoke. "Cherulli takes a South American for a flock of green stones. He doesn't pass along the stones. He's mobbed out. Dot Ellis is murdered, because maybe Cherulli's passed the stones to her. You go looking for this Donner guy, with the idea of taking him on as a partner and reforming the crooks of the world, and he's dead when you find him. You trap Ben Garren—and get a dick to shoot him before he can talk. Ain't that sweet?''

I smiled grimly. "It was Donelly or Garren," I said. "I didn't figure Garren would take it so hard."

Phil swore. "You come out here—get out to Duquesne, chasing Carrie Donner. You get the dope on her in New York. The Widow is carved up. And next Butman gets it. You tell me you chase Carrie into town. Steiner's with her—and when she lets go at you she gets him. Somewhere along the same time she hits you over the head with a fizz bottle. A guy you think is Quirt because he says he's a private dick tails her to the Harris House. She's mobbed out just as you and the guy you think is Quirt, for no particular reason, get there. Is all that fairly close?''

"Fairly," I said, grinning.

He got up from the chair, swore, turned his back on me.

"I've got a hunch you're a damned liar, Mal," he said. "I've got a hunch you're holding back on me. But I'm too much of a gent to even let you suspect I figure that way."

I kept on grinning. I was holding out Virgie Beers. She counted big, but I didn't feel that Dobe should know that. I wanted him to know enough to help me, and not enough to hurt me.

He turned around and faced me. He was frowning.

"You think all these killings are because a nightclub wop trims a sucker?" he asked.

"It's the best I can think—just now," I said. "Every once in a while the big guys preach a lesson. Boys and gals get taught to keep school. Sometimes the new kids get a worse dose than they rate. That's up to the big boys."

Phil grunted. "You're using words, and you don't know what's what," he sneered.

I nodded. "All right—I'll admit I haven't learned much. But we got the one that finished Dot Ellis."

The city editor grunted again. "You stopped a guy from talking—a guy who *could* have talked," he said.

I nodded again. "Any suggestions? I might get a microscope or try adding and subtracting figures for the secret formula. Or I could hop a rattler back to New York, furnish an office with thick rugs and etchings by Navarro—and mastermind from the inside."

Phil sat down again. I poured myself a drink, drank it, made a face. Dobe smiled with his lips.

"It's better when it gets down," he said. "What in hell did that fat widow and Chief Butman have to do with the green stones?"

I passed the bottle back to him.

"Anyone can ask questions. You can ask me fifty of them and if I can answer two I'll be lucky. But I'm still alive. This is 1930, and mobs work differently from what they did in Sherlock Holmes's time. I may stumble on something."

"On a slab in the morgue," he suggested. "Maybe you're right—maybe the killings are related. If they are, it isn't a bunch of green stones that's causing the gun-pops—"

The phone bell rang. I lifted the receiver, said that Howard Evans was speaking. I tried to make my voice sound sleepy.

Quirt said: "This is Jackson. No sign of my party. The front is loaded up with law—and I'd better ease away. What next?"

I looked at Phil Dobe. "Come back to the Penn," I said. "I'll wait up. I've got something to tell you."

He said all right, that he'd be over in twenty minutes. I gave him the room number and told him to come right up. He hung the receiver. Phil Dobe took out a gun that looked like a cannon and started inspecting it. I got up and walked around behind him.

"Don't mess things up like a damned kid," I warned. "Don't shoot until you can see the blue of his eyes."

Phil swore. "You do the talking, Mal," he said. "I'll be in the bathroom—and I'll get a look at him. He won't see me. If I'm crazy, and Quirt has sneaked back to town, I'll just sit tight. If he's someone else—I'll run the water."

I groaned. "He'll know I'm not alone," I said. "He'll be suspicious—"

Phil Dobe smiled. "Tell him this is one of your big nights," he said.

He took a small package from a pocket of his overcoat, hanging over the bed. He broke the string. The object inside was pink, soft, and laced. He tossed it carelessly toward the dresser.

"It's for my latest," he said. "She likes 'em pink."

I got up and swore at him. "How about a hat and a coat—if there was a woman in here—"

He chuckled. "Tell him she was in bed when she heard you were in town. She came right over—"

There was a knock on the door. It was soft, almost gentle. Phil's eyes widened. He headed for the bathroom door. I put the wine bottle out of sight, went over and opened a window, went over and opened the door.

She was very pretty in a dark, plain way. She wore a gray-black ensemble with a hat to match. Her face was pale and decidedly oval. There was no makeup. Her lips had slight color. She was rather small, weighed about a hundred and five or ten. Her eyes were dark and she kept them on mine. Her gloved hands were motionless at her sides.

"Mr. Evans?"

Her voice was low and soft. It had a smooth, almost soothing effect. When she spoke, a slight smile played about her lips. Her teeth were very nice.

I nodded. The door was half opened. She spoke again.

"Mr. Steiner sent me—he said you'd see me. It's important."

I stepped aside. She walked into the room. She stopped about three feet from the bit of pink silk. I shut the door and locked it. She didn't seem to notice the pink silk or the sound of the lock snapping. She picked out the chair Phil Dobe had been sprawled in, sat down, folded her arms casually. I went over and sat down on the bed, facing her. She had a small, flat, dark-colored purse on her lap. It was plain.

"How is—Mr. Steiner?" I asked.

She smiled. She wasn't beautiful, but there was a beautiful quality in her face. Her eyes held a soft expression.

"He's dead," she said very calmly. "He died about a half hour ago."

I reached for my package of cigarettes, knocked over an empty glass, picked it up. I offered the package to the girl. She refused with a slight smile.

"That's tough," I said slowly. "He was a pretty good fence. Maybe he should have stayed in his store."

She didn't seem to hear me. But there was no vacant expression in her eyes. They weren't even dreamy. She seemed to be looking into mine, through mine. There was a silence that was beginning to grow awkward when I broke it.

"And he sent you to me?"

She shook her head. "That wasn't the truth," she said. "I wanted to see you—and I thought perhaps that would get me inside the room."

I stared at her. She was smiling again. I started to get sore, changed my mind.

She said: "You're alone?"

She looked toward the pink silk even as she asked the question. I couldn't figure the best answer, so I stalled.

"Either way, it won't matter," I replied. "I'm curious."

She relaxed a little. She started to remove her right-hand glove, changed her mind, crossed her arms again. Her eyes were very beautiful. Her hat was a tight-fitting turban—there was no chance of seeing her hair, not as she faced me.

"I came to tell you some things," she said very quietly. "I'd prefer that you would just listen—and not ask about me. Do you mind?"

I nodded. "Of course I mind," I said. "But it depends on what you tell me."

She smiled, and the expression of her eyes changed. She seemed to be thinking.

"I'd like to help you," she said. "There are some things I can tell you that will help you. I'm sure of that. But I'm selfish. I must be protected. So you mustn't ask about me."

I leaned back against the wood at the foot of the bed and smiled at her.

"Sort of a mystery woman," I mocked.

She shook her head. "I'm not that important, I'm afraid. But I can help you. Do you need help?"

I couldn't figure her. So I played along. "What sort of help?" I countered.

She smiled with her dark eyes half narrowed. Her features were very perfect; her face was slightly too oval. She looked something like a Benda model I'd seen on the cover of some magazine. Only the mask-like quality was absent.

"You did rather a decent thing two years ago," she said. "Ellis wasn't much of a woman. You served two years for her. I think women admire that sort of thing, don't you?"

I kept my body relaxed, shrugged my shoulders. I thought of Phil Dobe, out of sight in the bathroom, thought of the man I knew as Quirt, on his way over to the William Penn. I tried to figure why this girl referred to Dot as "Ellis." She spoke again.

"Serving two years for a woman is something a man can do." Her voice was very steady, soft. "There are other things a man cannot do. Ellis was just one of Cherulli's women. She was very foolish. She was drinking in excess. Garren murdered her. You called in Donelly and when Garren attempted defense, Donelly shot him dead. That was foolish of you."

I kept my back against the wood of the bed, looked at the girl's gloved hands, looked at her eyes, smiled. I said nothing.

Her tone was one of casual conversation as she went on. "In prison you decided that a few very clever crooks were taking advantage of smaller crooks, weaklings. You decided to use the little crooks as the big ones did—and eliminate the big ones, the crime-breeders. I have the same idea, the same plan. I want to help you."

I nodded. I didn't say anything. She smiled almost lightly.

"My brother killed himself, after he had become so involved in dishonesty that there was no other way out. He didn't need money. That is the major motive of most criminals. But we had plenty of money. It was the adventure that he wanted, the thrill. After he died—I decided to do what I could. I have a lot of money to help me. I have information that will help you."

I leaned forward, tapped cigarette ashes into the tray on the chair. I didn't speak.

The girl said: "I can tell you why Ellis was murdered. I can tell you why Wirt Donner was murdered—and who killed him. I can tell you why and how the Widow and Butman were murdered. I can tell you why Cherulli was killed—"

She stopped. I half closed my eyes and blew smoke toward the ceiling.

She said: "Do you want to know any of these things? Are you interested?"

I shook my head. "You've got me confused with some other person," I said. "This Steiner—he must have given you a name similar to mine—"

She laughed a little. It was a very pleasant laugh.

"Mal Ourney is not at all similar to Howard Evans," she said. "But remember, after I got inside I told you that I did not come from Herb Steiner."

I nodded. "But perhaps he mentioned my name," I suggested.

She shook her head. She looked at her left wrist—I caught the gleam of a watch crystal.

"It's just one-twenty-five," she said in her same smooth voice. "Why not ask Dobe to come out of the bathroom?"

I got up and walked around behind her. She didn't move her body. My hands were shaking a little. I called out.

"Oh, Phil—come on out!"

He came out. The girl stood up, turned, faced us both. She nodded toward Phil.

"I don't know what the paper will do without you," she said softly. "But perhaps you can give me some suggestions to pass along."

Dobe looked at her, then at me. He said: "It's a frame."

I nodded. Dobe's right hand was under his suit coat. The gun bulged. The girl let her dark eyes glance toward the bulge. She looked at her wrist watch again.

"Your man Quirt's late," she said steadily. "He told me—"

She stopped as a very gentle tapping came into the room from the wood of the door.

· 12 ·

FOURTEEN
FOR ONE

I looked at Phil Dobe. "Go easy on that gun," I said.
"This'll be all right."

The girl kept on smiling. Her eyes were half closed.
I went over to the door, snapped the lock, opened it.
Two men were outside. They were both smiling.

The girl called out: "Hello, Ed—hello, Tom. Come
on in."

I forced a grin. "Sure," I said. "Come on in—it's
good to see you."

One man was short, with a thin face. The other was
medium in size. They both had dark hair and dark eyes.
They walked past me—both of them kept both hands in
their pockets. They smiled at the girl, but neither spoke.

I closed the door, but I didn't lock it. When I turned
around, Phil Dobe was standing near a window, his right
hand out of sight. He was smiling at the shorter of the
two men.

The girl remained seated. She said: "Mr. Grace and
Mr. Anderson—meet Mr. Ourney and Mr. Dobe. Mr.
Dobe is city editor of the *Post-Dispatch*. Mr. Ourney is
just visiting in Pittsburgh."

The two men nodded their heads. They looked bored. I didn't care much for the expressions on their faces.

I walked back toward the girl and sat near the foot of the bed again. Phil Dobe smiled in my direction.

"What's this all about?" he asked.

I shook my head. "Maybe we're supposed to guess," I suggested. "It's a new game, perhaps."

The girl got up from her chair, walked toward the door, stood with her back to it. The two men who had come in had separated. One stood near the bathroom door, the other had his back to the wall near the bed. They both had fixed smiles on their faces.

"We play it this way—" The girl paused, smiled pleasantly. Her voice was very nice.

There was silence, and then the sound of light footfalls came into the room. The sound ceased; there was a knock on the door. The girl looked at me. She said: "Quirt."

I nodded. I called out a come-in. My voice was fairly steady, but my throat felt a little dry. The door opened a short distance. The man I'd figured was Quirt came in. He looked around before he closed the door. He was smiling.

I spoke to Phil Dobe. "Yes—or no?"

He shook his head. "No," he said slowly.

The girl smiled toward the man I'd thought was Quirt, then smiled at me. She gestured toward the mild-faced one.

"You've met Mr. Christenson, I think."

I nodded. "He was a big help," I replied.

Christenson nodded. His mild blue eyes went around the room, then met mine.

"I'm glad, Mr. Evans," he said simply.

I said grimly: "The hell you are!"

The girl laughed lightly. Her laughter had a tinkling tone.

"Suppose we get into the game," she suggested. "We'll play 'Who's got the stones?' It's a lot of fun."

I nodded. "While it lasts, it is," I said. "What stones?"

Christenson spoke in his thin tone.

"By the way, Ourney—I think Virgie got away. Too bad."

I pretended I hadn't heard him. My eyes were on the girl's.

"What stones?" I asked again.

She let the smile fade away from her eyes and lips. But her voice remained pleasantly calm.

"The green ones," she said. "The ones Carrie Donner gave Garren. The ones you took away from him before you turned that dick loose on him."

I swore softly. "I'm sorry," I said. "But you've been given the wrong dope."

The shorter man of the two who had come in together moved restlessly. He muttered something I didn't get. I didn't like the sound of the muttering.

"Don't be silly." The girl's voice was still pleasant. Her oval face was turned toward mine. "Cherulli passed them to Ellis. Garren took them and got them to Wirt Donner. He sent them back by Carrie. Or maybe by Virgie Beers. Anyway, he sent them back. You got them."

I shook my head. "I can see why you *think* I did," I said. "But I didn't."

Christenson spoke. "I've got enough on him to turn him in," he said. "If he won't come through—let him squirm through a thirder."

Phil Dobe chuckled harshly. "It won't go," he said. "I know Mal—and I know the bulls in this town."

The girl turned her head slightly. She looked at Phil as though she were doing so for the first time.

"Ourney's a crook," she said steadily. "It doesn't matter that you're city editor of a scandal sheet. I'm fighting crooks. They ruined my brother's chance for a decent life. Every one I can send over—I'm sending over. I've got Ourney with the goods. He's been playing reformer. He's a crook."

Phil grinned. "Let me kiss your hand, madame," he intoned softly. "I think you're right."

The girl's lips got tight and thin. She narrowed her eyes. They were on Dobe's.

"I said I didn't know how that yellow sheet of yours would get along without you—and I meant it," she said softly. You talk too much. In a week or so you'll be quieter. You're playing with the wrong sort of children."

I sat up straight on the edge of the bed.

"Let's get down to facts," I said. "What's it all about? This fellow isn't Quirt. You want stones I haven't got, and you know things. Talk sense."

The girl walked over and stood close to me. She snapped the catch of her plain purse, got a hand inside. I looked for a gun—but it didn't come out. She made a swift movement and spilled green color all over the white spread of the bed. The color rolled in all directions.

Phil Dobe whistled softly. "Emeralds," he whispered.

The girl shook her head. "Fused glass," she contradicted. "I'm trading."

Christenson and Phil Dobe had moved in close to the bed. The other two men remained where they had been. The girl's dark eyes met mine.

"Trading—for what?" I asked.

For the first time there was a shade of annoyance evident. She didn't smile. Her voice wasn't so soft. She clipped her words a bit.

"For just *one* green stone," she said.

I reached into my vest pocket and produced the stone I'd picked up near Carrie Donner's body. I rolled it on the spread. The girl stopped its movement with a gloved finger. She didn't pick it up. She got her head down closer. The light was good, and the white of the spread made a nice background.

We all stared at the stone. I looked at some of the others. They were similar to the one I had found in the

Harris Hotel room. Most of them were larger. Some were the same size. Only one was smaller.

The girl straightened. There was a little gleam in her eyes.

"Thanks," she said. "That's all right, Mal. It's a trade."

She slipped the one stone in her bag. Phil Dobe looked at me.

"You don't have to stand for this, Mal," he said. "These crooks can't get away with anything like this."

I smiled. "You've got a good look at them," I said. "Don't forget them, Phil."

The girl went over to the door, turned her back to it. She had poise. Her tone was soft, amused.

"I'm letting you stay out of stir, Ourney," she said. "It's the best way—for me. My name's Jeanette Ramone." She spelled out the last name. "I'm registered at the Schenley. It's quieter there. I'll be there for a few days. I'm trying to do something in my way. You're a crook, but you're not important. I'm after the big ones—the ones who use the little fellows."

There was mockery in her voice. The last words were mine. I shrugged my shoulders, looked at Quirt.

"You saw me pick up that stone," I said quietly. "Congratulations."

He smiled at me. "I did the job you paid me for," he said. "I was in Quirt and Callarson's office when you phoned. I was on an extension. So I went over."

He moved toward the door. The girl looked at one of the two men who had come in together, then at the other. She nodded her head. They followed her.

The girl looked at me. Her oval face held a smile that was half mockery. Her voice was rather lovely. Softer than ever, perfectly controlled.

"Be careful of the glass, Mal—it's almost too pretty."

She went out. The others went out with her. The short, dark-haired man closed the door silently behind him. Phil Dobe took a step toward it; I caught him by an arm.

"Easy," I warned. "That quartet looked a lot like dynamite to me. It never makes any noise until it explodes."

Dobe swore softly. "They hijacked you," he muttered. "They're dirty crooks."

I shook my head. "Not dirty," I said. "That would be easy. They're clean, smooth. Damned smooth, Phil. I hate them when they're that way."

Dobe stared down at the stones on the bed. I counted them. There were fourteen. They looked pretty. I picked one up and studied it. It was larger than the one the girl with the oval face had taken from me. I liked it better.

"They hijacked you," Dobe muttered again. "And that bird Christenson—passing off as Quirt; he saw you—"

He stopped, his eyes narrowed on mine.

"You held back on me, all right," he muttered. "You didn't say anything about picking up that stone they grabbed. And you didn't say anything about this Virgie Beers."

I was frowning down at the green cuts of color. Phil Dobe kept walking around the room and muttering to himself. I scooped the green stuff up, went over to my bag, opened it up. I got out the stick of shaving cream, went into the bathroom, held it under warm water until it softened up. Then I shoved down the stones into the white stuff, one by one. The cream was held in a nickel container, and there was room for all the stones. I smoothed over the stuff at the top, ran the surface over my face a few times, wiped the skin off with a towel, held the cream under cold water.

Phil came in and watched me finish. He looked puzzled. I put the nickel cover on the shaving cream, put it back in my bag. I kicked the pink slip out of the way, got the wine, poured the last two drinks.

"I'm beginning to think you're right, Phil," I said slowly. "The green ice isn't the thing. It's just giving us a play. It counts—but not most of all. The killings aren't for the green stuff."

Dobe grunted. "You were damned careful with the glass that sweet-looking lady traded for the real article," he said.

I nodded. "Forget you saw anything green around here," I said. "Stick around fifteen or twenty minutes."

Dobe stared at me. "You're still holding back on me," he muttered.

I shook my head. "Virgie Beers is just another name to me," I said. "The thing's as thick now as it was at the start. But I think someone would like to frame me— in the right way."

The city editor grunted. "They heard you were going after the big guys—and that scared them to death," he mocked.

I shook my head. "I blundered into something," I replied. "I'm still in it."

"You're still blundering," Phil stated grimly.

I nodded. "That's all right," I said. "I know some people that can't move around enough to even blunder."

It was two o'clock when a lot of footfalls sounded outside the room. There was a knock—a pretty heavy one. I got up from my chair, told Phil to stay seated, went over and opened the door. Two dicks were outside. One looked like a dick—the other didn't. They were both middle-aged, and they looked as though they hadn't missed a meal in a year. One of them had a gray mustache; the other was smooth-shaven. They both looked at me and they both walked into the room.

Phil Dobe greeted the one with the mustache. "Hello, Landy. What's keeping you up?"

Landy stared at the city editor, frowned, looked around the room, frowned at me, coughed. His companion stood by the door and fingered a gold watch chain.

"Got a tip," Landy said. He looked at me for several seconds. "You Ourney?"

I nodded. "Out of the stir just a few days," I said. "But I didn't go up for robbing a bank. I stood a rap because women are the mothers of men—"

"Yeah," Landy cut in. "I've heard that, too. Nice, ain't it?"

"It's big," I said. "Bigger than all outdoors."

Landy made a noise that was something between a sniffle and a snort. He looked at the bed, then at the bag over in a corner.

"A guy named Malendez got taken for some emeralds over in New York not so long ago. We got a tip that the guy that had this room before you might have planted them here. We come over to look around."

"Nice to have your company," I told him. "The guy that had this room didn't have *my* clothes or bag—but you might look at everything, anyway. You never can tell."

"Thanks." Landy grinned at Dobe. "It's decent of you. You take the bed, Al. Make it right."

They did a pretty fair job. The best work was done around my bag. My overcoat got a lining pressing, and they were careful about the carpets, hangings and the two pictures in the room. It took almost a half hour. Landy had the shaving cream in his fingers, and the nickel cover off. But he didn't dig into the white stuff. His partner was breathing hard when they finished. Landy bit off the end of a cigar, lighted it.

"Hell!" he muttered. "Never had a tip yet worth a good goddam. But they're startin' to raise hell in New York about the Malendez stuff."

Dobe grinned. "Why?" he asked.

Landy shrugged his shoulders. "Maybe the stuff was worth more than they figured," he said. "All I know is that the chief told me to keep my eyes open. When this tip came through—"

He broke off, looked at me. I got a puzzled expression in my eyes.

"Where do I come in?" I asked. "I was in stir when they rolled this South American gent."

Landy nodded. "You were out when they started to fumble things," he said cheerfully.

"They?" I watched him relight his cigar. "Who's 'they'?"

Landy grunted. He brushed ashes from his coat with stubby fingers. He grinned at me, then at Phil Dobe.

"You know him well?" he asked Phil, letting his eyes flicker to mine.

Phil swore. "He was one of the *Post-Dispatch* chain gang, Landy. I know him well enough."

The detective widened his eyes on mine. There were little wrinkles running out from his lips.

"Nice training your sheet gives," he observed.

I leaned forward in the chair. "*You* wouldn't have guts enough to stand a rap for anybody," I snapped. "And remember, you haven't got anything on me."

Landy looked hurt. His companion made clicking noises with his lips pressed together.

"Don't get hard," Landy said. "We can take you along and *ask* you where the stones are."

He moved toward the door, followed by his companion.

Phil said: "You rate page ten on the search, boys. I'll use Landy's picture."

The detective who had run the job grinned. He opened the door.

"That's all right, too," he replied. "You've used worse faces."

They went out. I lighted a cigarette, inhaled, swore. Phil Dobe smiled at me.

"Getting fed up, eh?" he said. "Why the hell don't you pull out?"

I laughed that off. I was thinking of the girl with the oval face. And the bird she had called Christenson, who had posed as Quirt. I was thinking of the flock of stones she had planted—and the one she had taken.

"It's just getting good," I said grimly.

"For someone else, it is," Phil came back. "She grabbed off a money stone and planted a flock of glass. She tipped the bulls. Had just about time. She furnished a guy to stick with you until he saw something. She told you she could tell you a lot of things, but she didn't tell you a damn thing. You got taken."

I got up, went over and opened a window. The sky in the distance was red from blast-furnace flame. The cold air felt good. Turning around, I faced Phil.

"You interested?" I asked. "Want to give me a lift?"

He glared at me. "You know damn well I do, Mal," he said.

I got the shaving cream out of the bag, took off the nickel cover, got a nail file in the white stuff, and dug out a stone. It was fair-sized, had good color. The imperfection was slight, but easily seen. I handed it to Phil.

"A good jewel man can tell you what it's worth," I said.

He groaned. "I'm not an expert, but I can tell you right now. About a buck."

I shook my head. "If it's fused glass it's worth more than that. About seven or eight bucks. You may be wrong."

He chuckled harshly. "You're going crazy," he said. "I suppose that oval-faced kid came in here and traded you more than a dozen real emeralds for one, eh?"

I didn't smile. "That's what I'd like to know," I said. "She wouldn't gain much by planting fake stuff. The bulls wouldn't have me for anything."

Dobe narrowed his eyes and muttered to himself. He

wrapped the green stone in a corner of his lavender handkerchief and got out of the chair.

I said: "I think the bulls know something new on the Malendez case. You might have one of the bright boys look around at Headquarters."

He nodded. "Any other instructions?" he asked with sarcasm.

I nodded. "I'll see you at the paper—don't call me," I said. "Maybe, for once, you've got a decent reason for carrying that cannon of yours. Jeanette said she didn't know what the paper would do without you. She doesn't like your mixing in."

He went over to the door. "Hannelman's talking about making the office boy city editor," he said. "He could sign the advance slips as well as me—and that's the biggest job, anyway."

He went out. I smoked another pill, got undressed, called the Schenley, and asked if a Miss Jeanette Ramone was registered. I said that I was her uncle and it was important. I spelled out the last name. The clerk said Miss Ramone was registered.

While I was recovering from the shock he complained that the hour was late, but that if it were important he would ring the room. I told him to ring. After a few seconds I heard Oval Face's voice. It sounded a little sleepy.

"This is Uncle Mal," I said. "Sorry to awaken you, my dear. But I just wanted to tell you that the law was here. Their luck was bad. And give my regards to Cousin Christenson, will you?"

There was a little silence. She said finally: "I'm sorry, but there must be a mistake. This is Miss Ramone. You must have the wrong number."

I chuckled. "I'm getting closer to the right one, dear," I returned. "If you talk in your sleep don't mention any names."

She hung up. I did the same thing. I called the desk, asked some dumb questions, and learned that the man who had been shot in room 651 had been taken to the General Hospital. I called the hospital, said that I was a cousin of Edward Flynn, had just learned that he was in the hospital. I wondered if they could tell me his condition.

It took time and more explaining. Finally a cold-voiced nurse stated that Mr. Flynn was in ward B, that his condition was satisfactory, that he was sleeping easily, and that the visiting hours were two to three-thirty tomorrow afternoon. I thanked the cold-toned one and hung up.

I was sleepy, but I wasn't so crazy about the idea of sticking in the William Penn. There were a lot of hotels in town at which I hadn't stayed yet. One was two blocks away. I packed up, went down, and checked out. I took a cab and drove to the P. and L. E. station, got out, went through the station, came out at the other side. I didn't see anyone tailing along. I got another cab, was driven back to a corner about a block from the Waldron Hotel.

There wasn't much traffic. It was starting to drizzle. A dirty drizzle. No one followed me into the hotel. I registered as Elmer Christenson, was shown to a room on the second floor in the rear. The room was clean and the bed was hard.

The transom was opened—I closed it. There was a snap lock on the inside of the door—I snapped it. The shaving soap I tossed on the bureau with the brush. I got out a pair of green and white striped pajamas, washed, got into the stripes, got into the bed.

It felt good. I started to figure a few things out. I decided that Oval Face's trade had been a plant. She wanted me to have the green ice—and she figured that if she took the one stone Christenson had seen me pick up I'd think she was panning off glass for the real thing. She figured I was dumb enough to hang on to the stones— and not get them out of sight.

I didn't know whether Christenson had planted the one stone beside Carrie Donner's body—or whether she'd had it. Or whether someone else had planted it. The more I thought about the whole deal, the less sure anything became. There were too many outs. I was still strong for working on Virgie Beers. But she'd made a duck. Oval Face was too new to guess about. I wasn't so sure that anyone was running things—and yet I had the feeling that if someone wasn't running things, there was too much tough luck coming my way.

One thing was fairly obvious. Someone figured I was worth more alive than dead. There was a reason for that. I couldn't even get close to it. When I got to sleep, the drizzle had become a pretty heavy rain. It beat against the window glass. I dreamed about the girl with the oval face. And there was the old cliff that I was always falling over—always waking up before I reached anything. Sometime not far from dawn I fell asleep and didn't dream. That helped.

3

I slept until ten, shaved, ate a combination breakfast and lunch. The rain had turned to snow. It was a wet, clinging snow. I walked to the *Post-Dispatch* building, went upstairs. The staff hadn't arrived yet. Phil Dobe usually came in at about one-thirty. I got two papers from the files. One was an afternoon sheet, the other was the rival morning paper.

The police hadn't a thing on the mobbing out of Carrie Donner. They had a couple of humans who had seen the car speed around a corner. There had been no taillight, and neither witness had noticed a license. The theory was that it had been a revenge kill, but the police didn't seem to know what the revenge had been for—and they figured Carrie had got the dose for the same reason her brother had been shot out of things.

Herb Steiner wasn't talking; he was too sick. The whole thing came down to two facts: Carrie had been finished, and the bulls were in the dark. Herb had been shot in the belly—and the bulls didn't know what it was all about.

I read a couple of comic strips, learned that "Big Boy" Danver had taken one on the chin in the second session of his scrap with Kid Harpen, read that rum-runners had been stopped once again up around Detroit—and quit reading. I killed thirty minutes by watching a soprano make faces near the microphone of K.D.K.A.'s radio station, in the *Post-Dispatch* building. When I went back into the editorial room Phil Dobe was taking off his coat. A few reporters were around, waiting to get advance slips signed.

After that was done I sat on the edge of Phil's desk. He shook his head slowly.

"It beats hell!" he muttered.

"The weather?" I asked.

"That hunk of green." There wasn't anyone around, but he lowered his voice. "It's the real thing."

I grinned. "Sure," I said. "And so are the others. How much?"

"About eight hundred," he said. "Can you beat that?"

I nodded. "There're thirteen more chunks," I said. "Some of them are larger. Say ten grand for the lot. Not a bad trade, eh?"

Dobe grunted. "She did it with a smile," he said. "I don't like it."

I lighted a cigarette. Phil got a piece of newspaper from his pocket—a small piece. It was wrapped around something. He handed it to me.

"That's it," he said. "I'd rather you kept it around you."

"Thanks," I replied. "Don't suppose you've done anything on the Malendez case yet?"

"Wrong," he said. "I went down and had a talk with Reever. He's the chief of dicks just now. Next week it'll probably be someone else. Reever's getting too prosperous. Anyway, there's some fuss on about Malendez. Reever admitted that, but he wouldn't say just what. He gave me some advice."

I waited, but Phil didn't go on.

"Good advice?" I asked.

He shrugged. "Told me to keep a block or so away from one Malcolm Ourney," he replied.

I whistled a few bars of a popular funeral march. Phil didn't smile.

"He thinks I'm spotted?" I asked.

Phil shrugged again. "He didn't say that," he said. "He just told me it looked as though there was some hell breaking loose. He had a wire from New York. I got a look at the end of it. On his desk. Conelly sent it."

"Donelly, maybe?" I said. "You didn't get a look at the C, did you?"

"Maybe it was Donelly," Phil replied. "That's close enough, I guess. Does it help?"

I shook my head. "Donelly's a New York dick," I told him. "Every time I ran into him he was working out of his district. I figured that might be important. I'm sure of it now. Thanks for the ice job, Phil. I'll drop in later."

The city editor narrowed his eyes on mine. He tapped his barrel chest with the knuckles of his right hand.

"It's tough to quit on a job—but it's tougher to be dead," he philosophized.

"I'm going over to see a friend, at the General," I told him. "He didn't see something coming—and it hit him."

Dobe yelled for the morning editions, got a cigar going, swore at me.

"I hope *you* see it coming—and don't get hit," he said.

"Just to know you're with me in spirit—that's everything," I told him, and went away

·13·

BLACKJACK

I killed some more time and got to the General Hospital at two-ten. It was still snowing, and ore dust was dirtying everything up. The hospital was a depressing-looking building on a hill. It smelled like all hospitals and was a little more noisy than most.

I talked at the reception desk, talked some more at the third floor. A nurse with a poker face led me into a small ward. I spotted the bull reading a newspaper, half the way down. There were screens around some of the beds— and the nurse stopped at the foot of one.

"There's the patient," she said, and worked a mechanical smile.

I thanked her, moved around the screen. The bull came around and looked at me. Herb was lying with his back to me. He didn't move.

I smiled at the harness gent. "Reever said it would be all right," I told him. "Donelly wired from New York. Want to listen in?"

He shook his head and went away. Herb moved his head a little. He let his woman eyes rest on mine. They looked hurt and sad. His skin was soft and white. His lips were white.

"Hello, Herb," I said. "Sorry about it."

His woman tones were pretty faint. There was no expression to his voice.

"Like hell you are."

I smiled. "Let's let it ride that way," I said. "It's bad—when you get it in the stomach. How long you got?"

Hatred flamed in his eyes, then died. He mouthed nasty words, weakly, brokenly. His lips had no color. He looked bad—very bad.

"I'll get—over this," he muttered, after a while.

I shook my head. "Not in this crook's world you won't," I said. "You look bad, fence."

His eyes burned a little, back in their sockets. He was hating hard.

"You're through," I said grimly. "And the big guys are turning up Virgie."

It got him. He cried out, tried to pull himself up. Red splotched the white of his face. He was a crook—and I kept at it.

"She'll get life—maybe she isn't good enough on looks to beat the chair," I said. "They're turning her up for the Malendez kill."

He called me names. He was twisting around on the bed. The nurse wasn't in sight, but the harness bull came over. He frowned at me.

"What in hell you doing?" he demanded. "I got orders—"

"Virgie didn't—get him!" Herb Steiner was gritting out the words. He was fighting to get them out. "They're framing—her—"

I chuckled. It wasn't easy to do—not with the woman-faced fence dying on the bed. Even though Steiner was a rat—it wasn't easy.

"Yeah?" I said. "You can't help that any. You tried
to frame me. You got into my bag. Maybe Virgie didn't
get him—maybe I know she didn't. Hell'd freeze over
before I'd give anything of yours a break."

He sank back on the pillow. He coughed. The harness
bull grabbed me by the left arm.

"You gotta come away," he said. "I gotta have a
written order—"

I smiled down at Steiner. "You're going away," I
said slowly. "I'll give you a break. I'm after the guy
who got Wirt Donner. Give me the name—and I'll keep
off Virgie."

The harness bull gave me a jerk. Herb Steiner swore
at him.

"Let him—alone," he breathed weakly. "He ain't a
copper. Lay off, you bastard—"

The copper was dumb; he couldn't make up his mind
what to do. I bent over Steiner.

"Who got Wirt Donner?" I muttered. "Who's got
the Malendez stuff—the *real* stuff?"

His eyes were staring. The fingers of his left hand
plucked at the edges of a sheet—then relaxed, spread.
His face was white again, ghastly. His lips parted.

"Virgie—" he murmured, very weakly.

He started to cry. It was pretty bad. He reminded me
of Ben Garren. His eyes were getting misted, colorless.
He said again: "Virgie—"

I told the harness bull to get the nurse. He didn't want
to leave me. My right hand was near the bed, and Steiner
got a grip on it. Not much of a grip. The harness bull
ducked around back of the screen.

I said: "It's all right, Herb—it's all right. Take it
easy."

He stopped crying. I could hear the nurse hurrying
along between the rows of beds. Her rubber soles made
a light patter.

Steiner said very weakly: "The goddam—women—"

I tried a grin. He smiled a little. I guessed that he was thinking of Carrie Donner's rotten aim. His grip on my fingers relaxed. The smile went out of his face. His eyes were opened. His face looked like a woman's. He said: "Virgie—"

The nurse slipped around the screen, frowned at me, looked down at him. She touched his forehead, tried his pulse. She said: "He's dead."

I went away from the screen, and the harness bull followed me.

"I'll catch hell," he said. "If the chief didn't tell you it was all right—"

"What'll you catch hell for?" I asked. "Did he say anything?"

He was thinking that over when I walked out. I went down in the elevator, got out in another cold drizzle. I started walking toward the center of town. There was a choice; I could figure that Steiner had been answering my question when he'd used Virgie's name, or I could figure that he was strong for the blonde and was thinking about her last of all. She'd been in the boardinghouse when Donner had got the dose. She knew things. Maybe she'd liked Steiner.

I smoked three cigarettes on the way to Liberty Street. My hunch was getting stronger. Malendez had been taken for a lot of stuff. I had fourteen chunks of green ice— and Oval Face had at least one chunk. But it was small stuff. Between ten and fifteen grand. Dot Ellis, Angel Cherulli, Wirt Donner, and Carrie Donner. They hadn't been shoved out just because. Steiner had got it accidentally. Ben Garren had made a mistake. I couldn't figure the Widow and Butman. But the first four counted. Virgie Beers, the girl with the oval face—Christenson— they were still doing things.

The big guys? The girl who had given her name as

Jeanette Ramone—she had brains. She had poise. Maybe she was one of them. Christenson or whatever his name was, maybe he was one. I didn't think so. But they were sitting in.

I couldn't decide what to do next. Coffee and pie didn't help much. I kept thinking about the girl at the Schenley. After a while I decided to get it over with, took a cab out, and went into the hotel.

It was nice inside. She had a room on the third floor, and when I used the room phone she answered it.

"This is Uncle Mal," I said. "Just a social call. Can I come up?"

She said: "You may—Christy's here."

I told her that was all right, hung up, got into an elevator. She'd acted almost as though she'd been expecting me. I got out of the elevator and went down the corridor whistling shakily. The nearer I got to the room, the worse I felt. There was something about the oval-faced girl that jiggled my nerves. She was terribly sure of things.

2

Christenson opened the door. He gave me a gentle smile, gestured toward the far side of the room. A table light was on, but the place was dark. I went in, spotted the girl taking it easy on a divan between two curtained windows. She was in negligee, but it was a perfectly modest one. A rich black. She smiled at me.

"Hello, Mal," she said. "We were rather looking for you."

I picked out a chair that faced the divan. The girl's face was pale; her lips were almost colorless. I guessed that she was in her twenties, but couldn't be sure. She looked more like a Benda mask than she had hours ago. But her eyes hadn't enough color. She wasn't beautiful.

"I dropped over to tell you three things," I said. "The

first is that your story about the brother who erred was touching but silly.''

Christenson came in from the small corridor that was almost a part of the room, crossed to a chair about ten feet from the divan and almost opposite mine, and sat down. His face was expressionless.

The girl said: ''And the second?''

I smiled. ''I mentioned it over the phone last night. The dicks looked around nicely, but the green stuff wasn't there.''

She nodded, a little smile playing about her lips.

''It was there, but they didn't find it,'' she corrected. ''All right, Mal. And the third?''

''Herb Steiner just went out, up at the hospital. He told me things.''

She took her head off the pillow—sat up jerkily, got her right hand part of the way to her throat, let it fall back to her side again. She dropped her head to the pillow. Christenson leaned forward in his chair.

''He was a dirty fence,'' he said slowly and almost tonelessly. ''Too bad, Ourney—you can take the drop for that.''

I shook my head. ''I don't carry a rod,'' I said. ''And I used a cloth on the one Virgie tried to plant.''

The girl was breathing a little heavily. She spoke in a low voice.

''Just the same—you can go through for it, Mal.''

I shook my head again. ''It would be tough,'' I replied. ''Might make it a family affair.''

Christenson got up from his chair, walked around the room, went back and sat down again. He touched his mustache nervously with one finger.

''Just the same,'' he said carefully, ''it's a bad spot for you.''

I looked at the girl. ''Supposing I were getting a little worried,'' I said. ''Can you suggest an out?''

She kept her dark eyes on mine for a few seconds,

turned her head and looked at Christenson, looked back at me.

"Yes," she said quietly. "You can come clean with the money stones."

I shook my head once more. "The only emeralds I've got are the ones you planted on me, and that's straight. If you didn't know that, I can't figure why you wanted me to take a pinch. The bulls would have got the big stones."

She smiled. "I didn't say you *had* what we want," she said. "I said you could come clean with the stuff."

Christenson swore softly. "You worked me as though you knew what you were doing, Ourney," he said. "Maybe you weren't satisfied with what you got. Maybe you wanted the small ones, too. Well, you got 'em."

I sat back in the chair. The girl with the oval face pursed her lips. After a few seconds she parted them.

"They won't do you much good, Mal," she stated softly. "Honest to God, they won't."

"Better dig 'em up," Christenson advised quietly. "We're beginning to attract a little attention."

I laughed at that. It wasn't much of a laugh, but it got by.

"You're too damn clever for that," I said. "When a cheap crook goes out it never attracts much attention."

The girl sat up abruptly. She leaned forward.

"Steiner was no—"

"Shut up!" Christenson snapped.

His voice was soft, suave again. He smiled toward me.

"We'll talk straight, Ourney," he said. "A lot of honest guys think it's all right to grab coin from a crook. Maybe you're no exception. Miss Ramone feels that she can do something for the weaklings, say—by getting at the big fellows. You have the same idea. Perhaps Miss Ramone is better able to succeed. Perhaps you have swayed slightly from your purpose. Cherulli was hardly a crook. With some feminine help he made a big killing. In emeralds. You were lucky. But as things developed you became a bit unlucky. Fifty thousand dollars is a good sum of money. We will pay that—for the stones we are anxious to locate. A trip around the world—''

''I get seasick,'' I cut in. ''I thought you said we'd talk straight.''

The girl sat up, swung her feet to the floor. They were small feet. Her body was a little tense.

''I'll talk sense,'' she said sharply. ''Cherulli and the Mullens mulatto got Malendez for all he had. They doped him and got him into the East River. They figured on a getaway, but it got too late. Cherulli was getting scared. The nigger went back on him. She got religion, or something damn close to it. He slipped the stuff to Dot Ellis, told her to get it to you without your knowing what it was. Just something to keep for her. He figured with you just coming out of stir the green ice would be safe. Maybe she talked—she was doped up a lot of the time. Ben Garren gave her the works, got the stones. Then you came along. You let some of the smaller stones slip away—and played that you were trying to trace the guy that got Wirt Donner. You figured that would put you in the clear, when the hunt got tight. You figured wrong.''

She stopped. Christenson nodded his head. I smiled at the girl.

''It's a nice story,'' I said. ''Even if it didn't happen that way.''

Christenson got up and stood near his chair. His eyes were narrowed on mine; his face was twisted nastily. He started to sway.

The girl said: ''Sit down, Christy—we're just talking.''

I kept my eyes on him, nodding.

''Sure,'' I said. ''Just talking.''

"I could choke it out of him!" he gritted.

"That's wrong," I returned. "You know damn well you couldn't."

He got a sneering smile on his face, stopped swaying, sat down. I looked at the girl.

"Get on with the story," I suggested. "What happened next?"

She smiled back at me. There was a little color in her lips now.

"Underground got working," she said. "Garren got word that Wirt Donner and you were going straight and then some. You were going to do some cleaning up. Virgie Beers was his girl. He told her to get Donner. She refused. So Herb Steiner did the job. Did it and went over the roofs. That was before you got to Garren and the stones."

I nodded. "What next?" I asked.

She straightened on the edge of the divan. Her oval face had a nasty twist to it.

"It won't hurt you any to know what isn't news," she said. "I'll play with you, Mal. It's all right."

"It's for your brother's sake," I reminded.

She nodded. "For dear old Jerry's sake," she said. She sighed theatrically. "He was so damned innocent."

Christenson muttered something under his breath. The girl got her dark eyes on mine again.

"Carrie Donner and Virgie headed for Pittsburgh— Duquesne," she went on. "You traced them—and acted damn smart by pretending you were tailing them to find out things. You *knew* things—and you *had* things. But it was nice, Mal."

I nodded, "*I* thought so," I said.

She looked at Christenson, then back at me. Her tone was expressionless.

"You planted the little stones on Carrie, figuring the big guys might be close. They were. They drummed out Carrie, and you played along by grabbing one stone and acting as if you had something important. You took that city editor in—that was a good bet. That brings it up to date, Mal.''

I laughed at her. "You're skipping," I said. "How about Chief Butman and the Widow, in Duquesne? How about Red Salmon, in New York? And how'd *you* get the stones you say I planted on Carrie Donner?"

"Easy. Salmon was framed by Herb. Butman and the Widow—that was something else again. He carved her up, tried to steer the reporters off because he was yellow. Some of her hunky pals got organized and quieted him."

I nodded again. "And the stones you traded?" I asked.

She shrugged her shoulders. "I got them from Carrie before she was spotted out," she said. "Better come through, Mal."

I stood up, pulled my overcoat around, sat down again.

"It's a nice story, Miss Ramone," I told her. "Some of it's true. You do it pretty well. In the right spot it's a bad story for me. I guess you know the right spot. But the only stones I've got are the ones you tried to frame me with. If that had worked—where was your out?"

She wasn't smiling. "For the tip on the big stuff we'd have got you off with a ten stretch," she said.

Christenson shifted in his chair. He smiled at me.

"Fifty grand'll keep you in socks, Ourney," he said. "The stuff is hard to handle. You've done one stretch. Better be good."

I looked at the girl. "I'm sorry—but you've tailed the wrong gent," I told her. "For your brother's sake I'd like to see you get the stuff and grab off the big guys. But I'm helpless."

Christenson stood up again. The girl got up, too. Her lips were twitching. She motioned toward an alcove. Christenson smiled at me, moved something around in the right pocket of his dark-colored suit, came over close to me.

"With certain changes—the story Miss Ramone told

you is the one the New York D.A.'ll get," he said. "Better be good."

I swore softly. "There was a harness bull listening in on Steiner's last chat," I told him. "Don't rush things."

"Just—easy like," he muttered, and took his right hand out of the pocket.

The first blow caught me under the left ear. While I was on the way down he used the blackjack twice, hard enough.

I heard Oval Face call out harshly. "For God's sake— Chris—easy!"

I was on my knees when he hit the fourth time. It caught me just over the nape of the neck. The last thing I heard was the voice of the oval-faced girl.

"Jeez, Chris—go easy!"

·14·

BEDROOM STORY

She sat on the edge of the bed and patted my forehead gently with a towel that felt cold and good. I could see a portion of the room in which Christenson had black-jacked me down—but I couldn't see Christenson. My head ached all over.

"Damn him!" she breathed fiercely. "He shouldn't have done that."

I smiled a little. "He shouldn't," I agreed shakily. "It won't get him anywhere."

Her oval face was pale in the faint light of what seemed to be an alcove bedroom. I lay motionlessly and watched her blink back some tears. She saw I was watching her, moved the towel over my eyes. Her fingers touched the skin of my face. They were soft, nice.

"He knew it wouldn't—get him anything," she said. "He just—got sore."

I nodded. It didn't help the pains in my head any.

"Smash me open much?" I asked.

She shook her head, taking the towel away from my eyes.

"He had it wrapped," she said. "You've got some

bumps—but they're coming down. He just wanted to hurt.''

"He did," I told her. "But not enough. You can't tell what you don't know.''

I saw that she didn't believe that. Her eyes lost some of the sympathy they'd held—they held a hard expression.

"Better come through, Mal—" she warned.

Her voice trailed off. I sat up against the pressure of her right hand on my chest, felt better than I thought I'd feel. I braced myself with both hands, looked at her. In the dim light of the bedroom she was almost beautiful.

"Give it to me straight," I said. "What have I got— that you want?''

Her dark eyes narrowed on mine. She didn't speak. I looked at her.

"Where's Christenson?" I asked.

She got off the bed, went a few feet away, sat down in a low-backed, ornate chair. She reached somewhere inside her negligee and showed me an automatic. It looked like a thirty-two. It wasn't equipped with a silencer.

"Chris went out," she said quietly. "He's got things to do. But that doesn't help you any. A good lawyer kept me outside of walls—the last time I used a gun. It can happen again.''

I pulled myself back until I could brace my head against the wood that rose above the covers. I smiled at her.

"That's right. Maybe it was the lawyer—maybe it was your looks. I don't remember the case.''

"It didn't happen in this country," she said simply.

Her body jerked a little—she looked confused, then mad. I nodded.

"Maybe they're more sentimental in South America," I suggested.

She tried to appear puzzled. I asked her the same question again. "What have I got that you want?''

Her voice was hard. "Listen, Ourney—we played along

with you. Now we're working against time. Chris wanted to give you more of the same dose—when you came out of it. I got him away. You owe me something."

I felt the raised places on my head. They hurt when I touched them.

"Maybe," I agreed. "But what?"

She shifted slightly in her chair. There was anger showing in her eyes now. She held the automatic in her right hand—but she didn't hold it loosely.

"You did for Herb Steiner," she said slowly. "I can turn you up for it."

I tried a chuckle. "You know damn well you can't," I told her.

She was breathing heavily—her lips made almost a straight line. I could see the curves of her body. She was nice to look at. She smiled suddenly.

"You're tough, Mal," she said. "You're hard to get along with. But I like you, just the same. Supposing you and I made a duck for it. I know a nice place near Ligonier, up in the mountains—"

I kept my eyes on hers, scraped the fingers of my right hand over a cover, kept quiet for several seconds.

"Just the two of us—" Her voice was soft, persuasive. "Jeez, Mal—we could have it nice."

I nodded a little, keeping my eyes on her oval face. She was breathing heavily.

"I know a cabin up there—it would be worthwhile—"

"You're beautiful," I cut in, and put everything I had into the words. "But I can't see it, kid—"

"Just the two of us—" she repeated. "Listen, Mal— I'm sick of all this. It's too tough—for me. It isn't my racket. The first time I saw you—"

I never took my eyes from hers. "You make it sound like something," I breathed. "You wouldn't cross me up?"

She leaned toward me from the chair. The skin of her face was soft, close to mine. She was making it nice.

"Cross you up? God, Mal—I'm sick of this! Up there we could forget the whole thing. I know a way out—for just—the two of us."

"Chris might—find us," I said slowly.

She shook her head. "He won't. I swear he won't, Mal. And the others—they won't. You know who I mean. It'll just be the two of us—up there—"

"You're—making it sound pretty," I said, keeping my eyes on hers. "A fellow'd be lucky—"

"Mal!" She was very close to me now. "Don't you—want me—"

I took my left hand away from the bed covers and gripped her right wrist. My right hand went for her throat, got a grip, swung her off the chair and to the bed. She tried to scream—and choked. I got part of my body weight on her body, twisted the automatic from her fingers, got my left hand on her throat, too. She was gasping—her body was twisting. I tightened the grip of both hands.

Her eyes were staring into mine. I eased up a little on the grip.

"If you—yelp—I'll finish the job," I warned, breathing hard.

Her body relaxed. There was appeal in her eyes now. Waves of dizziness swept over me—the effort was a tough one.

"Once more—" I whispered—"what have I got—you want?"

She started to shake her head. I moved the fingers of both hands. She twisted—and I tightened the grip. Then her body relaxed again. I loosened my grip, kept my eyes close to hers.

"The big ones—the five—" she breathed weakly. "The green ones—that count."

I looked away from her, toward the other room. Five emeralds—that counted. Big stones—money stones. She wasn't lying now, I knew that.

"Where did Christenson go?" I asked.

There was sudden fear in her eyes. She lifted fingers and tried to take mine away from her white throat. I shook my head.

"You were trying to cross me," I reminded her. "Now come through. If you don't—"

"He went—to make—arrangements—" Her voice was weak, rasping.

I felt sorry for her, but I didn't show it.

"What arrangements?" I asked.

"Funeral—for Steiner."

I stared at her. "How does Herb figure?" I asked.

She didn't want to answer. I shifted my position, swung both legs over the side of the bed, pulled her head close to mine.

"Don't stall," I gritted. "Sure as Christ—I'll finish you—"

"He figures—big," she said. "He gets—a big ride—"

I loosened my fingers, took them away from her throat, picked up the automatic. It was a thirty-two. She lay back on the bed and rubbed her throat. She wasn't crying.

"Chris'll—kill me," she said brokenly. "He'll kill me!"

"Maybe," I agreed. "Or maybe I'll do the job first. It all depends on your answers. Don't hold out—just answer. Don't lie. I can tell about that. Some of the answers—I know. Who shot Wirt Donner?"

She opened her eyes and looked into mine.

"Herb Steiner," she said in a whisper. "I gave it to you straight."

"Why?" I asked.

"He didn't know—until after he'd told Virgie Beers the game—that she was playing with Herb, too. He was afraid—he'd heard Donner was going straight—"

I remembered Steiner's last words. They had been a repeated name—Virgie's. She had played with both Stei-

ner and Wirt Donner. And Ben Garren—she had been
at his place.

"Where did Steiner come in?" I asked.

She hesitated. "He was just out, you know that. He
handled things—"

I smiled a little. "It's too slow," I said. "If Christenson comes back here—I'll kill him. I'll have to. Talk
fast—and I'll get out. You can come—after you talk—
if you want."

She nodded. "He'd kill me," she said again.

I believed that. "Cherulli and the Mullens mulatto took
Malendez for a lot of green ice," I said. "They shoved
him in the East River, over at New York. A boat's
propeller smashed him up. What did they get?"

She moved her head, looked toward the outer room.
There was dull fear in her eyes. The fingers of her right
hand were still at her throat.

"You've got to let—me get away," she breathed.

I nodded. "I haven't *got* to—but I will," I told her.
"After you talk. What did Cherulli and the mulatto get?"

"Plenty." Her voice was better now, clearer. "The
five big ones—worth fifty grand apiece. I've seen two
of them—"

"Where?" I cut in.

"Puerto Colombia, down in South America. That's
where the green stones come from—most of them."

I nodded again. "You and Christenson were tailing
Malendez—down there?"

Anger showed in her eyes.

I said: "Don't do that—talk! If I get my fingers on
your throat again they'll stay there until you're out."

"He got clear—we came up. He was playing the clubs
in New York. Mostly Angel's place."

"Who sent you down to South America?" I asked.
"You and Christenson—you're out of New York."

She nodded. There was no color in her face.

"I don't know—who sent us down," she said. "That's

straight. Christenson had plenty of coin—we did things right. Someone down there had a tip on Malendez. He was spending a lot. He was showing the green stones—talking.''

She broke off, shuddered. Her eyes went toward the other room.

"Who's Christenson?" I asked.

She shook her head again. "He's hard, cold," she said. "I met him in Chi. He damn near killed me when we let Malendez get out of Colombia, got up here too late. He *will* kill me—''

"Cherulli got yellow," I interrupted. "He passed the stuff to Dot Ellis. She was to get it on me, and I wasn't to know that I had it. Then, when things blew over, she was to get it back. She talked—and Ben Garren went after the stones. Where did he come in?"

She narrowed her dark eyes. "Chris knew him," she said.

I swore softly. Christenson was important. He had worked Garren against Cherulli and Dot Ellis—and Wirt Donner. But Steiner had been more important. "You got fourteen stones—the ones you traded for the one I picked up near Carrie Donner's body," I said. "How?"

She didn't want to answer that. I moved my right hand a little. Fear caught her. Fingers could hurt, and silence.

"You had Chris trailing Virgie and Carrie Donner. Virgie made a getaway, inside the hotel. Chris got to the Donner woman. She had the little stones. He got most of them—then he called you."

She nodded. "He bossed the mob-out job?" I asked.

She said slowly: "I don't know. Even if you kill me for it—I don't know."

I got off the bed, backed away a little shakily. I felt bad. My whole head was sore, aching. My eyes weren't clear.

"Somewhere between Cherulli and Carrie Donner—five stones were lost," I said slowly. "The big stones.

Fifty grand each. That's what you and Christenson think I've got?''

She nodded. ''I planted the stones, the little ones, on you. He called the bulls—using some dick's name. A New York dick, I think. He figured you'd give us the plant if he made a play to get you off. It didn't work.''

I smiled. ''Not quite,'' I said. ''You've been a good girl, keep it up. How about the Widow—and Butman?''

She shook her head. ''Something else,'' she said.

I stared down at her. ''I think that's your first lie,'' I told her. ''Somehow I'm letting it pass. I don't get much kick out of fighting women. You're too clever to be a fool. Get clear.''

She sat up a little, took her hands away from her throat.

''It's a cinch—to say,'' she said. ''Ever try—getting clear?''

''What's your name?'' I asked. ''If I can ever get you a break—''

She shook her head. ''That's no good,'' she said. ''Listen, Mal Ourney—no matter what happens to me, you take your own advice. Get clear.''

''With Herb Steiner's funeral coming up?'' I said grimly.

She narrowed her eyes on mine. ''Take the stuff— and get clear,'' she said. ''Maybe you can pass it. Anyway, it's pretty. But don't stick. You're a target—now.''

I smiled at her. ''You're not going to tell Christenson you talked like this,'' I said. ''You haven't got the guts.''

She shrugged. ''He'll get it out of me,'' she said. ''He always does.''

I swore. ''Tell him I choked you cold—when you came out of it I was gone. It's the best out. Give me a name—the name of someone bigger than Christenson—''

She shook her head slowly. ''I can't, goddam it!'' she breathed. ''The name's covered. I wish to God I could, Mal. I know about the Ellis thing—that was white. I killed a guy because he wasn't white. I'm pretty damn crazy over you, Ourney. But I'm tangled up—I can't get clear—''

I took the bullets out of the automatic, tossed it to her.

"You've got more. Fix it so it looks right," I told her. "I suppose you'll stick. It's rotten business, but it's your business."

I backed toward the outer room. Her oval face was white in the semi-darkness of the alcove.

"Get out of this, Mal," she called weakly. "You got yours—don't stick—"

I went out. It took me twenty minutes to get back to the Waldron Hotel, and I spent most of the time trying to separate lies from truths. After a while I gave it up. It was too difficult, with my head feeling the way it did. And anyway, figuring out things didn't seem to be getting me anywhere. I liked a lot of the girl's story. But there was too much missing. That was the part I didn't like.

2

I had an hour's nap, used up six grains of aspirin, kept my head under cold towels for a half hour, went out and had soup that didn't taste good—and headed for the *Post-Dispatch* editorial rooms. It was dark, but fairly clear. There was a snap in the air, and Liberty Street was crowded with people quitting work.

Phil Dobe was at his desk. He didn't see me coming in. I was almost behind him when a voice reached me from somewhere behind a large file case. "Hello, Ourney—how's things?"

I knew the voice. It was Donelly's. He stepped around and smiled at me.

"Pretty good," I told him. "Not that you give a damn, but just to answer the question. How's business?"

"Rotten," he said. "Not that you give a damn, but just to be agreeable."

Phil Dobe swiveled around and frowned at Donelly. He spoke to me.

"He's been digging for information, Mal—I didn't give it. But I couldn't kick him out."

I smiled at Phil. "Donelly's all right—from the neck down. And sometimes he has good ideas."

The New York dick turned his red face toward the city editor.

"Knew you'd worked here once, Mal," he said. "Tried all the hotels, then came over. This gentleman was so dumb I knew he was expecting you sooner or later."

Phil Dobe got up out of his chair and moved up close to Donelly.

"Listen, bull," he snapped, "in this town I can knock a New York copper cold—and the local force will cheer."

Donelly grinned. "The local outfit might cheer if you *could* knock me cold," he said.

I shoved in between them and told Phil that Donelly was a good guy, that he wasn't important enough to be bad, and that he'd killed a guy for me once. Phil grunted.

"Oh, Garren," he said. "Well, maybe he was dumber than I am."

Donelly started to say something, but I took him by the arm and we moved away from Phil's desk, over toward the rolltop used by the dramatic critic. That gentleman was absent.

"Anything special?" I asked. "Or just a trip to the west?"

Donelly kept smiling. "Got a wire telling me you were out here," he said. "And some things have been happening. Thought I'd come out. How was your grandfather, over in Boston?"

I grinned. "He was out skating," I replied. "So I didn't wait for him to come back. When he skates—he skates."

The New York dick nodded. "He must," he said. "Who got Carrie Donner?"

I kept on smiling. "Still asking questions, and still working out of your district, eh? Who got Herb Steiner?"

Donelly frowned. "Eat with me—dutch treat," he said. "I'll tell you some things."

I said that would be all right, and went over to Phil's desk. I talked low.

"Went up to the Schenley—was offered fifty grand by that oval-faced kid and the bird I used as your man Quirt. The fifty was for a trip away. They think I've got five hunks of green ice worth fifty thousand a hunk. I said no—and Christenson blackjacked me out. Then he made a duck. When I came out of it the girl held a gun on me and tried to vamp me into telling her about the emeralds I haven't got. I played up and got her by the throat. She talked some, and some of her story sounded fair enough. Part of it not so good. She said they were going to give Steiner a funeral, and that he was a pretty big guy. Sort of running things. When she started to lie, I said so long."

Phil made marks on a piece of copy paper with a blue pencil. He whistled softly.

"Steiner was dead—when you went up there?" he asked.

I nodded. "I broke the news to them," I told him. "They tried not to—but they took it big."

Phil swore softly. "Watch your step," he warned. "How about this dick?"

I shook my head. "Yes and no," I said. "We're going to feed together. Anything new on the Butman-Widow kills?"

He shook his head. "It's almost dead," he said. "Maybe it doesn't count in this other thing, at that."

I said maybe, but I wasn't convinced it didn't. Phil called me back as I turned away.

"You were around when Steiner went out," he said. "One of the boys got a pretty fair description from a nurse. Did he say anything?"

"Not a thing," I said. "He was pretty sick."

Phil grunted. "Yeah," he said. "He must have been feeling badly—just before he died."

I told him I'd see him later, and waved to Donelly. The red-faced one followed me out. We went along Liberty until we came to a wop eating place.

"Like spaghetti?" I asked.

Donelly nodded. "If I don't have to wind it around a fork," he replied.

I told him he could eat it with a spoon if he wanted to; and we went inside, picked out a table in a corner, and ordered. When I took off my hat Donelly swore softly.

"You have tough luck with that head of yours," he said.

"It feels that way," I told him. "Steiner's a crook; did you know that? Or he was one. I butted into a party he was on—and he slugged me down."

The dick grinned at me. "To hell with the fairy tales," he said, "Let's play nice and count the lies out."

"All right," I replied. "Anything been happening in the big burg?"

He shook his head. The waiter came along with clam chowder for me and bean soup for Donelly.

"It was so dead that Lentz asked me to look you up," he said. "I read a good book on the way out."

"That's great," I told him. "Don't tell me the name— I've read a book."

Donelly groaned. "There weren't any jokes in the one I read so bad as that," he said. "It was all about a guy who tried to reform crooks. In the end he just got himself killed. Ain't that hell?"

I inhaled chowder, listened to Donelly doing the same in a bigger way with his soup, and smiled at him.

"And you came all the way out here to tell me that, eh?" I asked.

He scattered a flock of oyster crackers in his soup and

shook his head. I used up some more in the chowder. They went good.

"Where'd Virgie get to?" he asked casually.

I found a clam, tried it out without liquid surroundings, and was sorry.

"I was going to ask you that," I told him. "I wonder."

He got a little sore. "Listen, Ourney—some things have turned up in the Malendez case. He had more stuff on him than we thought. They're raising hell down in a godforsaken spot called Puerto Colombia—"

"Any place where they grow green stuff isn't godforsaken," I cut in. "Don't get sore, Donelly."

He put down his spoon and looked at me with narrowed eyes.

"What kind of green stuff?" he asked.

I grinned at him. "Apples, tomatoes, lemons—that sort of stuff. Great agricultural country, Donelly. Ever been down there? What women!"

He leaned forward in his chair. "The day I took you down to see Lentz," he said, "there was a guy saw him after you. Herb Steiner. Know what he told him?"

I shook my head. "Too tough," I said.

Donelly smiled with his lips. "He said he figured you were out to get him. He said he was worried. He said maybe he'd get out of town."

I leaned back in my chair, and the waiter took the soup plates away. When he'd gone I looked at Donelly.

"Well?" I said.

"You did the job," Donelly stated. "Now it's up to you to do another."

I thought that over. Then I said: "What sort of a job?"

Donelly smiled more broadly. "A little squeal job. Maybe we can fix it so we'll forget the Steiner thing."

The waiter came along with the spaghetti. Donelly cut his with a fork. I frowned at him.

"This way—" I said, and worked the stringy stuff around the prongs. "By the count—one, two—"

"To hell with the comedy!" he snapped. "You're in a bad spot, Ourney. I told you to keep off. You mixed in—"

"You're out of New York State," I interrupted. "Take it easy."

"I can get the papers—and take you back," he snapped.

I laughed at him. "The spaghetti's damn good," I said. "They tell me Cherulli's old place served it up nice, too."

Donelly swore. His face was redder than I'd ever seen it. But he got control.

"The trouble with you is you don't believe what you're told," he said.

I leaned over toward him. "Neither do you, Dick," I said. "That evens things up."

·15·

DONELLY

We didn't get anywhere at the wop joint. After coffee I
said I was going back to the paper, and he said he'd
come along if I didn't mind. I told him it would be all
right, paid the check, bought cigars, and led the way
out. He stuck pretty close. We got near the *Post-Dispatch*
building; there was the usual bulletin hung behind the
glass that showed up the working presses. Donelly swore
softly.

"Hell!" he muttered. "Look at that one!"

I looked. There had been a hundred-thousand-dollar
fire over on the South Side. That led off. A couple of
nervy yeggs had cracked a box in a branch post office
in a nearby suburb—and had got away with some stamps.
A Wilkinsburg society girl had jumped from a third-story
window in her home. She'd been badly bruised. A town
called East McKeesport hadn't any water supply because
the pumping-station engine had gone bad. And one Herbert Steiner, reputed to be a New York gangster, was to
be given a big funeral, it was alleged. He'd been shot
in a room in a local hotel, and the police were still looking
for the killer.

I read the last item twice. Donelly chewed on his cigar, muttered something about seeing my editor friend. We went in and upstairs. Phil Dobe was reading the *American Mercury* and cursing to himself. We went around near him. He looked up from an article titled "Pittsburgh— Steal City."

"Mencken's getting soft," he stated. "He believes newspaper reporters. Burke wrote this one. I can't figure when the hell he got sober enough to do it."

Donelly leaned over and looked at the magazine.

"Who in hell's Mencken?" he asked.

Phil grinned. "Played second for the Pirates, five years ago," he said. "Came up from the old Orioles, down in Baltimore. Got run off the team for using split infinitives in a pinch."

Donelly looked puzzled. "It's a baseball magazine?" he muttered.

I nodded. "You wouldn't like it," I told him. "No pictures."

Donelly swore at me. Phil tossed the magazine aside.

Donelly said: "You got a bulletin up—Steiner is to get a floral display for the finish."

The city editor nodded. "Nathan and Dirring gave it out," he said. "They're doing the embalming."

I lighted a pill, getting rid of a half-finished cigar that didn't suit.

"How come the bulls let the body loose?" I asked.

Phil grunted. "He won't keep," he said. "They know all they want to know."

Donelly smiled grimly. "I'd like to believe that," he said. "Who's putting up the coin for the funeral?"

Phil shrugged. "I've got a man trying to find that out," he said. "The morticians won't tell."

I grinned. "Just like daisies," I said.

Donelly frowned at me. It was a cinch that he was suspicious of both Phil and myself.

The city editor swiveled around, got out of his chair.

"I'm going out to eat," he announced. "I was waiting for you birds to finish, so I wouldn't have to pay the check."

He went out. I sat on an end of the desk and looked at the dirty floor. Donelly lighted what was left of his cigar and kept on frowning.

"I don't get it," he said. "Herb Steiner was a cheap fence. He don't rate a procession—not by a damn sight."

I thought of several things, but kept them to myself. There was no way of telling how much Donelly knew.

"If you didn't get him, Ourney—who did?" Donelly asked suddenly.

I passed that one. "Maybe he wasn't so cheap," I said. "And maybe you know he wasn't."

He looked puzzled. "I'm going out to this Nathan and Dirring place," he said. "Where can I reach you?"

I grinned at him. "Which means you haven't got anything on me," I said. "I'm at the Waldron. Under the name of M. Christenson."

I watched him closely, caught the faint flicker of surprise in his eyes. It told me something.

"Why Christenson?" he asked, and tried to make his voice casual.

"No reason," I replied. "Just a name I saw in the phone book while I was looking up a number. Liked it better than my own."

He smiled almost pleasantly. He said he'd look up Nathan and Dirring, go out and try to find out things, then come back and look me up. He said we were both after the same thing—and he thought we should sort of stick together.

"Sort of," I agreed. "But just what is the same thing we're both after?"

He grinned. "Try and guess," he replied, and moved toward the phone booth at the rear of the editorial rooms.

I sat on the desk, watched him come away from the

shelf near the phone booth and go out. He waved to me. After a few minutes I called up the Schenley and got Oval Face.

"Still alive?" I asked.

She said that Christenson hadn't come back yet.

"Maybe Herb didn't have 'em on him," I said.

There was silence. Then she said she didn't understand me. I told her that was all right, that I was just thinking out loud. Her voice was a little shaky. She said that a key was in the lock, and that "he" was coming. Her voice got low and more shaky. I told her to talk as though she were calling some female friend.

She started to talk about some kind of face powder, told me to wait a minute. I waited. At first I couldn't hear much—then things got louder. I heard a voice that sounded like Christenson's, pitched high, call her names. The phone made noises—she called shrilly. "No—for God's sake, Chris—"

After that I didn't hear anything. I held the receiver to my left ear, waited. Ten seconds passed—there was a faint click. I stayed with it. Central said my party had hung up. I told her to ring the number again. Christenson answered. His voice was steady. I tried to change the tone of mine.

"Donelly—from New York headquarters," I said. "When can I see you, Chris?"

He swore softly. "Any time, Ourney," he replied. "Come on up."

He hung the receiver. I did the same. I talked to myself.

"There's just one thing I *won't* do," I said grimly, "and that's come on up."

2

I got back to my room in the Waldron at ten o'clock, after a pretty long talk with Phil Dobe. I used the key going in, and found Donelly lying on the bed and looking comfortable. He grinned at me.

"The lock was easy," he said. "Nice beds, eh?"

I told him I'd tried a lot of hotels in town, and the Waldron beds were as good as any. He seemed cheerful.

"Saw Mr. Dan Dirring," he said. "He didn't want to talk at first, but later he did. Not a bad fellow. A brother Elk. Learned the undertaking business in my hometown, Brooklyn. That's not far from New York."

I looked interested. "I've heard of the place," I said. "I've always meant to go there."

Donelly stretched his legs comfortably. He had small feet for a dick.

"It seems that Herb Steiner left a request, in the form of a note on his person, that he should be buried in the Furnaceville Cemetery. Ever hear of the place?"

I nodded. "It's back of Duquesne—about eight miles," I said. "Used to be some blast furnaces there. Abandoned now. Think the Duquesne plant has a slag dump around the spot."

Donelly nodded. "A pal of Steiner's named Andrees is coming on to see that things go over big. Steiner salted away his coin, and he had a yen for a final show. Hearse leaves the mortician's place at three tomorrow afternoon. A lot of flowers, and five cars for friends."

Donelly grinned at me. I grinned back.

"Who's going to ride the five cars?" I asked.

Donelly shrugged. "It's funny as hell," he said. "What's the game, Ourney?"

I sat down in a chair and put my feet on a windowsill. The window faced an alley. I shook my head.

"I don't see any game," I told him. "Steiner was rated as a cheap fence. But then, he worked pretty smoothly until he was grabbed. He made coin. He wanted a nice funeral—and he fixed it so he'd have it. The cars may not be loaded with his pals, but the flowers will be there. A lot of crooks have had the same hunch on funerals."

Donelly kept on smiling. "The local coppers are looking for Virgie Beers," he said. "They think she knows plenty."

I nodded. "So do I," I said. "But she isn't one of the big guys, Donelly."

His smile faded a little. "Maybe the big guys'll be at the funeral," he said slowly.

"There'll be a dick or two present," I said. "Maybe the big guys'll think of that—and keep clear."

Donelly frowned. "It's a hell of a note," he muttered. "I can't figure it."

I looked out at the alley. "You're not doing badly," I told him. "Look at all the things you've found out."

He sat up and scowled at me. He got sore in a hurry.

"I've found out enough to pull you back to New York!" he snapped.

I laughed grimly. "What good would that do?" I asked. "You're after green ice—and cold enough without it. You'd make yourself a joke."

He glared at me. "You know too much," he said. "If you know what I'm after—you're worth taking back to New York."

I laughed again. "Listen, Dick," I told him, "the Malendez job is no secret. Every copper in New York knows about it. Angel Cherulli got to Malendez for maybe forty or fifty grands' worth of emeralds. He did in Malendez—but he's been mobbed out for trying to hog things. It just happened he tried to work the stones off on me."

Donelly swung his legs over the side of the bed, kept on scowling.

"You fixed it so I had to shoot Ben Garren out," he said. "I didn't know it at the time, but Ben had the stuff. You were there when I got there."

I nodded. "I didn't fix anything," I said. "I didn't know what it was all about. All I knew was that Garren had lied to me about a woman. The woman had been present when Donner was finished—she was Virgie Beers, the blonde. Garren said he didn't know her. When I caught him in a lie, I went up to Ossining and got hold of a cab driver who told me things. I gave it to Garren straight, and he wilted. You got him before he got you, that was all."

Donelly grunted. "And you got the Malendez loot before I got there!" he snapped. "And it was worth more than any forty or fifty grand!"

I widened my eyes and stared at him. I tried to act.

"Hell!" I muttered. "So that's what the fuss is about!"

He smiled nastily. "Don't pull that surprised stuff on me," he advised. "A fence getting a big show before he goes under dirt doesn't throw me off, Mr. Andrees."

I swore at him. He kept his eyes narrowed on mine. His face was red and splotched.

"When you get off the coke—go up in the Hill district and try arak," I suggested. "You'll have bigger and better dreams. Me—Andrees?"

The New York dick smiled with his lips pressed together. He parted them.

"Just that," he said. "You're trying to work a throwoff. Maybe you blundered into the stuff—maybe you didn't. But you got the ice. You know what it's worth. You're not a cheap crook, and when you get tired holding the stuff, and the bulls are beginning to forget, you can have the big ones recut. And you can cash in. You're throwing a big funeral for Herb Steiner, trying to make the bulls and maybe some other guys think he was a wiser guy than he was. A bigger guy. You want a lot of people to believe that he got the big stuff—and planted it. And you're doing it all under the cover of being a goddamed reformer—a white guy out to protect little crooks from big ones."

I took a deep breath, exhaled heavily. I grinned at him.

"Lean back and rest," I suggested. "After that speech you must be tired."

He got off the bed, stood near it with both hands in hip pockets. He looked pretty sore.

"No banging me around," I said. "My head's bad enough right now. And you've got brains enough to know it won't work."

He smiled. I didn't like the smile.

"I don't work that way," he said. "I'm a good guy."

"Yeah," I said. "You got a confession out of Red Salmon—and he knew as much about the Donner kill as you do about the Malendez job."

Donelly made a noise with his lips. He sucked in air with them almost pressed together. He stood staring down at me.

"Listen, Ourney," he said slowly, "I'll give you a break. It would mean a lot to me to grab the Malendez stuff and get it back to New York. Lentz would see that I got a shove up the line. You know this town. You know Duquesne. You just admitted you know this cemetery. You're a cool guy. You don't have to work on a shoestring and get rid of the stuff right away. That makes you hard to get. You worked smoothly—you were in stir when Cherulli did the job. You came out just at the right time. Come through—and I'll let you jump the country. I'll put it on Steiner."

I lighted another pill. "That's another nice speech," I said. "But it doesn't mean a thing. If you had anything on me you wouldn't make that proposition. You can't take me across the state line until you get extradition papers, and you can't get papers unless you've got something on me. You're a nice dick, and you use a rod sweet—but you just don't count with me. Take a walk— I'm going to bed."

I stood up and started to take my clothes off. Donelly stood near me, moving his fingers nervously.

"Get going," I said, "or I'll call the house dick and tell him there's a man in my room annoying me."

He wanted to step in close and hit me, but he had brains. He worked a smile that was pretty fair.

"I'll tail you until you get sick of looking at me," he stated.

"If that's the case, you should have quit an hour ago," I replied.

He went out, slamming the door. I waited fifteen minutes, went out in the corridor and looked around, came back into the room and called Phil Dobe.

"Anything happen in the way of murders?" I asked.

He said that everything was quiet, but that if I had any advance information on a kill he'd like to get a cameraman on the job. He wanted to know what happened to Donelly. I told him that he'd gone away for a while, but that I thought he'd stick in town. Dobe said that the Steiner funeral was to get away from the Nathan and Dirring parlors at three tomorrow afternoon. He said he'd have a man covering the procession. He said he thought Steiner was a Jewish name, and he didn't know what it was all about. I told him that maybe Steiner had been a Christian, and he said that it didn't matter a hell of a lot anyway—the worms wouldn't be able to make any distinction.

We hung up and I remembered that Donelly had been in the room when I'd come up. I opened my bag, shoved some shirts out of the way, and looked for the stick of shaving cream. It was about where I'd put it. I took off the nickel cover, stood up, and stared at the cream. It was all messed up. Something sharp had been used on it. The green stones were gone.

3

At eleven-thirty I rode down in the elevator, spotted Donelly reading a paper in the lobby, stayed in the elevator, and went down to the basement. I got out a side

entrance and walked out of my way three blocks before
I reached the *Post-Dispatch* building. Donelly wasn't in
sight when I went up. Phil Dobe had gone out—I found
him drinking coffee in a restaurant next door. He was
alone. I sat down across from him and gave him all the
late news.

"Donelly got 'em," he said. "What a guy you are—
telling him your hotel."

I ordered some coffee and argued that point.

"I'm after more than the small stuff. My play is to
hold open house, in a way. If Donelly went through my
stuff and had brains enough to dig into the shaving cream,
why didn't he take me in? He had something on me."

The city editor grunted. "He's giving you rope," he
said. "He thought maybe you wouldn't check up and
see what had happened."

"Why didn't he do a neat job—and fix the soft stuff
the way it had been before?" I asked.

Dobe smiled. "You rushed him—by coming in," he
said. "He didn't figure you'd come along so soon."

I shook my head. "He was lying on the bed—he
looked real cozy," I replied. "Maybe he didn't do the
job."

The city editor swore softly. "Who did?" he asked.

I shrugged. "*You* knew where the green stuff was,"
I told him.

He straightened, stared at me, swore again. I grinned
at him.

"Just because that's stolen goods—don't grab for it,
Phil," I warned. "I'll turn you up—"

He chuckled, poured coffee from his cup to the saucer,
and drank it noisily. The waiter brought mine and I got
rid of some of it.

Dobe said: "Donelly figured you were working this
funeral. What's your guess?"

I groaned. "I don't like it," I said. "I'd like to stay

away. But that won't help. I've got a hunch there'll be others there who'd like to stay away. This doesn't look like one of those processions where it's any fun going for the ride.''

Phil smiled faintly. "Did Steiner have a woman?" he asked. "Really?"

I shrugged. "Most men do have," I said. "You think someone's trying to draw her in?"

He shrugged. "If he had a woman and she loved him enough—she'd take a chance on a lot of things to be there when they toss in the dirt."

I nodded. "It looks like something should break— along the line," I said. "Donelly is all wrong when he figures I'm running the job. But maybe he's not so far off on the reason. That oval-faced kid said that Christenson went out to arrange for the funeral. She was getting hurt when she said it. I don't think she lied. Donelly seemed to know that name—Christenson. I told him I registered at the Waldron that way. It was the truth, but it sort of hit him. Whoever is bossing the processional— he figures on people being there. People he wants around. It looks tough.''

"It looks like news," Dobe muttered.

I smiled grimly. "I was a good guy, Phil—but don't lay it on too thick. I'll scribble some lines and mail 'em to you tomorrow morning. They may make things simpler.''

The city editor looked at me sharply.

"If you feel that way—stay off," he said. "If you go for the ride—take my gun along."

I told him I'd think that over. I said I'd go along. I told him I couldn't get the oval-faced girl off my mind. She was pretty nice.

He whistled softly. "What was her name?" he asked. "Jeanette Ramone?"

"That wasn't it," I replied. "Maybe Mary Smith or

Nellie Jones. What the hell does a name matter? She was just roped in, I'd swear to that."

Phil grunted. "It's a bad time to get soft—and mix with a woman," he warned.

I nodded. "That's the way it usually happens," I said. "At a bad time."

"She's a crook—whether you like her or not," Phil said. "Don't slop over."

I finished my coffee. "A lot of women are crooks," I said. "All of them haven't the guts to get it out of their systems—and go right."

Phil regarded me suspiciously. "A crook's a crook," he said. "Don't waste sympathy."

I nodded. "Every case is individual," I said. "News is news—but you don't use all of it."

He swore at me. "For Christ's sake—don't get technical," he muttered. "Start theorizing—and you'll get lead in your lungs while you're thinking up nice words."

"Just the same," I said, "I'd like to know how she squirmed loose from that mess. My hunch is that Christenson's a bad guy to fool along with. She made a mistake. He doesn't act like a man who likes mistakes."

Phil frowned down at his empty saucer. Then he grinned.

"I've got a gun and a bottle of pretty fair Scotch at the flat," he said. "The gun's real—and you can have it all. The Scotch has only been cut twice—and you rate half of it."

I shoved back my chair. "I rate it all," I told him, "but half will be just about right. Let's move."

4

It was cloudy, smoky, and cold—the next morning at ten. I got up with a slight headache and six hours of something that might have been loosely termed sleep behind me. I had a hot shower with a cold rubdown and dressed slowly. I looked over the service Colt that Dobe had given me. The idea of packing the rod was good—and bad. I thought it over—and decided to pack it.

When I went outside, with the Colt pretty bulky in my right overcoat pocket, Donelly was standing near the elevator smoking a cigar. He grinned at me.

"You get up late," he said.

"I got in late," I told him.

He nodded. "About four," he said. "I waited up."

I pressed the button. Donelly looked pretty bad around the eyes.

"Nice day for a funeral," he observed.

I nodded. "I'm not going along," I told him. "I'll send flowers."

He narrowed his eyes on mine. The elevator door opened and we got inside and dropped. We got off, went into the lobby.

"Going out of town?" Donelly asked.

"Got a toothache—going to look up a dentist," I said. "Want to come along?"

He shook his head, smiled at me, and drifted toward the leather lobby chairs. I went outside, lighted a cigarette and watched a young fellow in a dark coat come out and yawn. I headed toward Smithfield Street, and after three blocks went into a cigar store. The young fellow in the dark coat strolled past; he didn't look inside the cigar store.

I went out, walked back toward the hotel, turned off, went into the nearest drugstore, and had a fizz to help my head. When I came out the fellow in the dark coat was across the street looking in the window of a florist shop.

I went up to the corner and bought an afternoon paper, just out. There were a couple of sticks on the Steiner funeral. They were written with considerable irony. Flowers were piling up at the funeral parlor. They were from well-known gangsters in Chicago and points east, according to the cards. A lot of the names were obviously fictional, the reporter felt. The news item ended up by giving the time and starting place of the procession, and stating that the police were still working on clues, and soon hoped to grab Steiner's killer.

I read the paper standing near the corner, went into a phone booth, and called the Schenley. A desk clerk informed me that the Ramone apartment had been vacated at nine—and that no forwarding address had been left. I called the Waldron and had Mike Donelly paged. He came to the phone.

"When that young chap in the dark coat comes back and tells you that I lost him somewhere around the William Penn, don't bawl him out," I told Donelly. "You know how it is."

He chuckled. "It's just fun, Ourney," he said. "And say, if you're riding along, after you get the tooth fixed, you'd better lose that rod somewhere."

I hung up. Donelly was no fool—the tighter things got, the more convinced I was of that fact.

But I kept the service Colt. The fellow in the dark coat followed me along to the William Penn. I didn't go in. I went around the corner, snagged a cab that was cruising, and told the driver to make time getting to the Point. The chap in the dark coat was left flat-footed. There wasn't a cab in sight. He just stood on the corner and watched me go. We were held up by traffic a block away, and he started to trot along in the direction of the cab. We got going, and the last I saw of him he was standing on the curb trying to hail cabs that didn't have the vacant sign showing. Seven blocks away I stopped the driver, told him I'd changed my mind, paid up, crossed the street, and went into a picture house.

It was eleven-forty. The picture was something about two women and a man, and the dialogue was just rasping enough to keep me from thinking. One of the women looked something like Virgie Beers. In the end she was shot accidentally by the man she loved. She took a long time dying and I walked out. I wasn't very hungry, but I went into a lunch place and had ham and eggs. It was a few minutes after one.

·16·

FUNERAL

I caught the two-fifteen train for Duquesne, tried to read a paper on the way out—and got off at the station at three o'clock.

The town looked as dirty as ever—mill smoke was blowing back toward the crest of the slope beyond the river. I spent thirty minutes moving around the hunky section of town and asking dumb questions about the Widow Gunsten. The answers weren't worth much. Some of the men had forgotten her—several had never heard of her. One mill worker grinned and said he didn't blame the chief of police.

I found that Monkerson was the big burial gent in the hunky part of town. He had a frame building on a corner, down near a section of the steel plant walls from which a lot of pounding sound was drifting. His place was ore-dust-stained and had faded flowers in an urn at each side of the entrance.

I went inside and didn't breathe too deeply. There was a heavy odor of some sort of disinfectant. The reception room was small—and there were other rooms beyond.

Except for the pounding from the plant the place was very quiet.

After a short time there were footfalls. A fat, short, prosperous-looking individual appeared from the rear. He smiled at me. He had blond hair and blue, shining eyes. He wasn't even slightly cadaverous in appearance. His eyes questioned me.

"I should like to rent a car—not a hearse," I told him. "One of your funeral cars. One with curtains. Dark color, of course. I'll want it for about three hours, with a driver. I should like the driver to be middle-aged. I'll pay fifty dollars for the use of the car and should like the matter to rest between us."

His shining eyes narrowed a little. He smiled and his face became almost cherub-like.

"You go where with the car?" he asked directly.

I smiled. "To the Furnaceville Cemetery," I said. "Herbert Steiner, an old pal of mine, is being buried. I want to be there—but I don't want to join the procession until it gets close to his final resting place. I will instruct the driver."

He nodded. "Fifty dollars—" he questioned slowly.

I got out the money, handed him two twenties and a ten. I told him where the hearse was starting from and asked him how long it would take to reach the cemetery gate. He said he thought about an hour and fifteen minutes. He said it would take my driver about twenty-five minutes to get me to the same spot. That meant we'd have to leave at about four, to be safe. I looked at my watch—it showed three-thirty-five.

I told him I'd go out and dig up some cigarettes, and he smiled and said the car would be outside when I got back. I went out, walked two blocks, and got my pills. I asked the heavily mustached store proprietor if the police were making any headway on the Butman and Widow Gunsten murders. He grinned, showing bad teeth, and shook his head.

"What for dey do dat?" he asked me back. "Him an' she—dey bot' bad."

I nodded, lighted a pill, and went out. I walked back toward the funeral parlor of Mr. Monkerson slowly. Five stones—worth fifty grand apiece. That was all right. Emeralds could be worth that much and still not be marked jewels. They'd be large stones, beautifully colored, very transparent. They'd have to be perfectly cut—emerald cut. Something like a coffin.

I thought of Carrie Donner, stopped at a dirty lunch place, and got a phone. I called the Pittsburgh morgue and was told that the body was being held for relatives who were coming on from New York. Outside, I headed for the funeral parlor. When I got there, a dark sedan with curtains down was at the curb. A tall man with gray hair and eyes stood near the rear door. He smiled at me.

"This my bus?" I asked.

He said that he guessed it was, if I was going to the Furnaceville Cemetery. I told him I was going there— and that I'd tell him where to stop when we got out near the main gate. He smiled cheerfully and opened the door.

I got inside—the door shut. It was dark. As I reached for a curtain, there was pressure against my right side. Gun-muzzle pressure. I heard someone breathe sharply.

"Sit down, Mal—sit down." It was a voice I knew. "We're both going to the same place."

I sat down. The car started, getting through the gear speeds smoothly. I looked toward Virgie Beers. In the faint light of the car's interior she seemed pale, worn. Her eyes looked very bad. They were puffed. She kept the gun muzzle against the material of my coat. The car was climbing a hill.

"I was inside when you came in," she said. "Heard you talking to Bright-eyes. I tripled your fifty, and he let me ride along. He went for a walk and I got inside first."

I nodded. "You look like hell, Virgie," I said.

She smiled. "I feel worse than hell," she returned. "But not so hot."

I relaxed. "Take the rod off," I suggested. "It isn't right to act that way on such a sad occasion."

Her body stiffened. I saw her face twist. I was sorry, and I told her so. She took the gun muzzle away from my side, pulled up the curtain on her side about two inches. It made things a little brighter.

"I was over at the hospital—when he went out, Virgie," I said. "It wasn't so hard. He used your name twice— the last words he used."

She was crying a little. The car kept climbing the hill behind the steel plant. I was silent for a few minutes. Virgie was quieter now. She started to swear.

"The dirty, rotten crooks!" she breathed. "The bastards! If I had half a chance to get—"

She went on, and I didn't stop her. She used nasty words, and she put a lot of feeling behind them.

After she got through I said: "Carrie got him, you know. She was trying for me."

She nodded. She laughed bitterly.

"You don't know what it's all about," she said. "You just blundered along."

I nodded. "You tell me," I said.

She swore at me. "The hell you don't know what it's about!" she snapped. "And when this party's over *I'll* know—and you won't give a damn. You won't be alive enough."

I didn't like the way she said her lines. It sounded like the real thing. I turned my head a little and looked down toward her left side. She leaned forward and swore at me.

"Keep your head up, stoolie!" she snapped. "I'm not on a bed this time—and I'll shoot you right to hell!"

I turned my head away. The funeral car had stopped climbing and was running along on the level, in high. The road was fairly smooth.

I said slowly: "I wasn't in on Carrie Donner's murder, Virgie. I was tagging along—but I got there too late."

She made a sucking sound with her lips. They looked white.

"Don't whine, Ourney," she said. "You're getting yours, along with the others. To hell with the green ice! I'm getting square!"

I started to reach for another cigarette, but she told me to take my hands away from my coat pocket. She got the rod Phil had given me, stuck it somewhere on her side of the car. She was getting worked up. I had a hunch she was hopped for this ride. It looked nasty.

"Ratted it, you did!" she muttered. "Got to Wirt Donner in the Big House, told him you were going to go after the big guys, show the little ones what suckers they were. Told him you needed help. And Wirt was fed up with the way he'd been kicked around, framed. He fell for it. All the time you were working with 'Tip' Christenson and that slimy moll of his!"

I sat back and kept quiet. It was coming straight now, and I knew it. Virgie was putting on this show—and she was pretty sure of things. She was hopped up enough to brag. I was to go out—and she just didn't care about keeping anything quiet.

"They let Malendez get away from them, down in South America. They sent Cherulli a code wire—and Angel got working. He used Babe Mullens for the pretty stuff. Then he figured that Tip and that egg-faced brat were too far away to count. He didn't know they were steaming in close. So he finished off Malendez and got the stuff. He didn't know that you were coming out, and wise to the deal."

I swore at her. "You're crazy!" I said. "How could I be wise—in stir?"

She laughed harshly. The funeral car was speeding now. The tires made a shrill whirring sound over a good road.

"How does any crook get wise to what goes on outside?" she asked. "You knew, all right. You knew that Angel was hogging things. He wasn't going to split. And Herb was outside ahead of you—he knew, too. He got close to Dot Ellis, and she lied just enough. Garren stuck with Angel, even though you were working on him. He figured that Dot was going to double-cross Angel, after he'd passed her the green stuff. He got her—but the job was done. He got the little stuff—she'd shoved you the money stones."

I leaned forward and looked at her. I tried to keep my voice steady.

"Like hell she had," I said.

She was getting excited. "Herb gave your pal Donner the stomach dose," she said. "Why not—wasn't he a dirty rat? Wasn't he working with you? You got the goods on Ben Garren—and called that bull Donelly in to shoot him down. Smooth, Ourney—Jeez, but you worked nice!"

I started to speak, changed my mind. The funeral car was running over a rougher road now. It was making more noise.

"Carrie and me—we were wise, all right. We worked with Herb—he went for your bag. The big stuff wasn't there. Herb figured maybe you'd gone copper—you was working with the bull Donelly. He made us duck to Pittsburgh, but we fed that fat landlady a number. You worked fast, Ourney—damned if you didn't. Wired that grafter Butman that we had some of the Malendez haul. He came over and raised hell. Carrie had the stuff—she laughed at him. He went back to the Widow's place and took it out on her."

"Why, Virgie?" I cut in. "Why'd he take it out on her?"

Her voice was pitched high, but the driver was separated from us by a partition of glass. And the car was running fast.

"You don't know!" she mocked. "You don't know—

the hell you don't! You knew the Widow was Carrie's sister. You knew that grafter Butman took her to Pittsburgh after he got on the bull force. And when she told him she didn't know anything about Carrie having green stones, he went hunky. He grabbed a knife—''

Her voice broke. I was staring toward the back of the driver's head. We weren't so far from Furnaceville now.

"Who got him?" I interrupted.

She shifted around in the seat. She got the gun muzzle raised a little.

"It won't hurt you to know," she said. "It won't hurt you to know anything. There's just one out for you. Carrie got to two coppers who wanted him out. They figured he was taking you for a ride. They put out red lanterns—and when the car stopped they let him have a Tommy load. Then they steered the reporters off. They're still doing it.''

I smiled grimly. I'd thought I was getting the women clear—out of the house before Butman got to them. And Carrie Donner had already fixed it for him. The Widow had been her sister—that meant the Widow had been Wirt Donner's sister, too. And when she'd refused to work on Carrie—and get the stones for Butman—he'd knifed her.

"He must have been hitting the booze," I muttered.

Virgie Beers laughed nastily. "He was always doing that," she said. "The bulls under him hated him—he was a dirty grafter.''

I nodded. My eyes met her narrowed ones.

"I didn't send him any wire," I told her. "Maybe he just was suspicious—and went over. He knew the Malendez job had been worked—he knew Wirt Donner had been in stir—''

She laughed at me. Her mouth was working a lot, and she didn't look nice. Her face was all splotchy.

"You tagged us—and we played along. Carrie figured you had the big stones—you were working a stall. I

wanted to stop it. Herb came out and you walked in
on the three of us. We were trying to figure things. You
got Herb by the throat, and Carrie let go. She missed
you—"

Her voice broke again. I didn't speak. Her voice was
hard when she started again. Hard and steadier.

"We had to leave Herb and make a getaway. You had
some of the mob down below. They tailed us. We split,
in the hotel—Carrie had the small stones. I got out the
back way, and I could hear the lead pounding, two blocks
off. Goddam you, Ourney—"

"Steady," I said as her voice started to shrill. "You're
messing things up. I wasn't in on that—"

"Don't crawl!" she shrilled. "You got the little stuff—
hogging it all—"

"Christenson got it," I said. "His mob finished Carrie. He came to me, tried to plant the stuff. He sent in
two dicks to get it on me. It didn't work. He figured like
you—that I had the big stuff."

She laughed hysterically. She was rocking a little,
beside me. The gun muzzle wasn't steady, but it was
close. Too close.

"You're yellow, Ourney!" she stated. "You worked
with Tip—don't I know it? And you'll get the dose with
him—don't I know that?"

I leaned forward and tried to figure an out. I knew
Virgie's story was straight enough. Only two things were
wrong. I hadn't sent the wire to Butman—he'd just gone
next door and made a good guess. Good—and bad. Bad
for him. And I hadn't been working with Tip Christenson. Two mobs, fighting for emeralds that were worth
big money—with me in between. And Virgie's show
ahead. I looked toward the back of the driver's head.

"You've got me wrong, Virgie," I told her. "I was
playing fair—trying to get at the big guys. I'll admit that.
You'll be rubbing me out for that—nothing else."

She swore harshly. "You're a yellow liar," she said.

"I told you there was an out—there is. You didn't get Herb—that's why. You can split with me. Me alone. All of the stuff. Big and little. That's the out."

I shook my head. "I've never seen the big stones," I said. "I had the little ones—someone grabbed them from my room last night."

She leaned back. I looked at her. There was a terrible smile on her splotched face. She coughed, and her thin body shook a lot. She rolled down the window on her side and tossed Phil's rod out. She got her body shoved into the corner opposite mine, with her gun muzzle toward my stomach.

"Don't try to grab this rod," she warned. "You're through, Ourney."

My mouth felt pretty bad. Dry. I tried to smile, but it wasn't much good. The driver turned, tapped on the glass. He couldn't see below our shoulders—the window glass was high. He pointed ahead.

We were running along near the Furnaceville Cemetery. The town was a few miles beyond. Ahead, some cars were moving; they were turning off the road, going slowly. There was the hearse. Then came three open cars, packed with flowers. Sedans followed—I counted four of them before Virgie spoke.

The driver had shoved aside the sliding window behind him. He looked toward Virgie.

"Follow in—keep a hundred yards back of the last car," she said.

He nodded, closed the window, slowed down. The last car turned in; I looked at the cemetery. It was pretty bad. Overgrown—gravestones slanting at angles. The road through it looked rough. The cars ahead were moving very slowly.

The driver pulled our car off to one side. Virgie told me to pull up the curtain on my side. I did. She was smiling bitterly as I turned my eyes toward an open grave, across a plot of grass. The cars had all stopped behind the hearse. Seconds passed. Then I could see men from the funeral parlor carrying the casket toward the grave. A minister followed.

Virgie said quietly: "Get out, Ourney."

I looked at her. Her eyes were narrowed and shining a little. I looked at her gun.

"Don't do it—Virgie," I said unsteadily.

"Get out, Ourney!" she repeated. Her voice was pitched higher.

I opened the door, got out. Other car doors were opening. Oval Face got out of the first one—the one that followed the last flower car. One man got out of a second car. Two men got out of the third. A minister was leaving the fourth. The oval-faced girl was in black; I didn't recognize any of the men. And then I saw Christenson, stepping clear of the second car.

One of the flower cars had pulled out of line. The fourth car pulled over near it. Men got out, went toward the hearse. They looked like the funeral-parlor men. They were moving the casket out now, taking it toward the open grave.

Virgie's voice sounded loudly. "The second car— Christenson!"

The oval-faced girl swung around. Her slim body was tense. Flowers spilled upward and outward from the flower car that had pulled out of line. Men rose, lifted Thompsons. There were two of them working the guns now.

I shouted toward the oval-faced girl, hoarsely: "Get— down!"

I was on my knees as the bullets tore into the second car. Dirt splattered near my right shoulder, splattered again near my head. It wasn't machine-gun bullets that kicked up the dirt—Virgie was letting go. I heard one of the sharp cracks from the car I'd ridden in.

Twisting my head, I saw Christenson stagger, near the second car. He ran several feet—turned, faced the flower car. The three other men whirled, swung up guns.

Sub-caliber guns. Christenson went down, was motionless. Two of his companions went down. The other was spraying lead toward the flower car. He did it for several seconds—then he dropped his gun, slumped to the earth.

Two cars came in through the gate—traveling fast. I twisted my head, saw them slow up. Men piled out of them. I caught a glimpse of Mike Donelly.

"Dicks," I muttered. "Donelly—coming in—"

The flower car was getting under way. It circled around the open grave, cut in toward the cemetery gate. Donelly's voice reached me.

"Low—let 'em—have it!"

Donelly's men turned loose their lead. I was out of line of the fire, but I could see things pretty well. It didn't last long. The funeral flower car shot off at an angle, stopped abruptly. A figure stood up, shouted something hoarsely, slumped back into the flowers.

I waited a few seconds, pulled myself to my knees. The oval-faced girl was lying fifty feet away. I could hear Donelly telling his men to get in close, but to watch themselves. I got up and went over to the girl who had called herself Jeanette Ramone. She was unconscious, but she moaned a little when I lifted her head. I got my coat under her—went back toward the car Virgie and I had ridden in.

She was lying back in the seat—a smile on her face. Her right-hand fingers held the gun—very loosely. I took it away from her. There was red over her left breast— her dress was opened. Two stones were on the seat beside her. Three were spilled on the floor of the car. They were big, beautifully cut—a rich green.

"Got—off?" she said weakly. "I hope—to Christ— Tip—didn't. He was—your—big guy—Ourney—"

I said slowly: "He didn't, Virgie. You had—the stones all the time?"

She shook her head. "No—good," she said very weakly. "I don't—know who—"

She stopped speaking and turned her head to one side, away from me. I thought she'd gone out, but she spoke again. She said in a whisper: "Herb—"

When I touched her left wrist there was no pulse. I left the green stones where they were, went away from the car. The driver was standing ten feet away, talking to himself.

"Jeez!" he was saying. "Jeez!"

He kept repeating the word as I went past him. Donelly was bending over Christenson. He straightened as I came up.

"Dead," he said. "Tip Christenson—all shot up."

I nodded. "Virgie Beers's party," I told him. "Her boys, in the flower car. I don't figure why—she's got the emeralds beside her. Shot herself. All through."

Donelly swore softly. "It's a big party," he said. "Some of 'em aren't dead—most of 'em are. A Tommy bullet hurts like hell."

I said again: "Virgie's got the big ice—in her car. Why she staged this party—"

He walked away from me, went toward Virgie's car. The minister was leaning over, talking to the oval-faced girl. I went over and she smiled at me.

"All right, Mal?" she asked.

I nodded. "Chris is, too," I told her. "He's dead."

She shuddered, got her hands over her pale face. People were coming toward the plot of grass, the cars. They were running. Donelly came back with the green stones in his hand. He stood beside me.

"Pretty as hell, this stuff is," he muttered. "Five of 'em, eh?"

I nodded. Donelly slipped them into a pocket. Men were crowding around asking questions. Donelly spoke to me.

"You and the girl stick close, Ourney. I got work to do. Got to get some of these guns to the docs, so they can get well, get lawyers, and get out to use Tommies another time. Stick around."

He moved off, giving orders as he went. The oval-faced girl was crying. The minister looked at me with a stupid expression in his eyes.

"It's terrible," he said in a stunned tone. "I can't comprehend—and that poor soul—over there—"

He gestured weakly toward the casket. I felt like swearing, but didn't.

"Herb's all right," I said grimly. "He'll keep a few hours longer."

2

We sat in my room at the Waldron—Donelly, Phil Dobe, and I. There was a little gin left in the glasses, none in the bottle. Five green stones rested on the table around which we'd pulled the chairs. Donelly looked at them and swore.

"Pretty, pretty!" he said mockingly. "Beautiful, fused glass. Malendez wasn't a complete sucker, at that."

Phil Dobe grinned. "When the Associated Press tapped out that dispatch from Puerto Colombia I got a big kick," he said. "Christenson never figured Malendez would work in the glass stuff. Not after the way that baby spent coin in South America. He was a playboy."

Donelly grunted. "You can't figure crooks—and you can't figure suckers," he said. "He had me fooled—leaving the money stones down there. Wise baby."

"It didn't save his neck," I reminded him. "They got him—Cherulli and the Mullens nigger."

Donelly swore softly. "And we've got her—in the big burg," he said. "Couldn't figure you for a while there, Ourney. Didn't know which way you were going to jump. Figured that big guy chase of yours might be a stall.''

I smiled. "The others did, too," I said. "No one was sure who had the big stones. Virgie must have checked up, learned these hunks were fakes. So she played along—until Herb Steiner went out. She must have had it bad for him. She went a little off her head, I guess. That final show of hers was put on to get us. Christenson and me—and maybe you, Donelly. The oval-faced kid, too. And Virgie damn near put it across.''

Donelly nodded. "Tip Christenson was a fool to show up," he said. "But then, so were you, Ourney. And so was I. Virgie figured we'd be that way. Steiner didn't rate a grand parade after his finish. He wasn't such a little guy, but he wasn't so big.''

"Christenson wanted to get close to Virgie—that's why he came," I said. "He had an idea about putting on a funeral for Herb, too. He wanted to pull Virgie in. The oval-faced kid told me that—said he went out to make arrangements. But Virgie had one of her boys there first. And she used more money on the job.''

Donelly grinned. "And I got the local bulls to let it go through, when I saw something queer was on the make," he said. "Give me credit.''

Phil Dobe swore. "We don't have to," he stated. "You'll take most of it.''

Donelly looked hurt. He narrowed his eyes on mine.

"I handed you a bum line in here last night, Ourney," he said. "I figured that if you knew why the funeral was being thrown, you'd come through to clear yourself, when I accused you. I said a lot of things that weren't just right.''

I nodded. "And you took away the small stones I stuck in the shaving cream," I said.

He grinned. "It was a nice hideaway," he said. "But I came early and worked slowly. Those stones are real—I checked them. Who planted them on you?''

"Christenson," I replied. "Then he tipped the local bulls. He wanted them to get me right—and then he was going to make a trick offer to ease me out of a stiff rap if I told him where I'd planted the big ones."

Donelly nodded slowly. "I believe that," he said. "Got any more stones?"

"Just one," I said. "I'll contribute it to the collection. Phil had it appraised for me—and I didn't shove it in the soap. What's new at the morgue?"

The New York dick frowned. "One of the boys with me went out," he said. "Two of Christenson's guns are dead. I don't know 'em. A guy named Scheafer, working for Virgie in the flower car—he won't use a Tommy again. The others'll come through, including one of the funeral-parlor gents. That makes four dead."

I swore softly. "Dot Ellis, Cherulli, Malendez, Wirt Donner, Ben Garren, the Widow, Butman, Carrie Donner—"

"For God's sake, cut that stuff," Donelly interrupted. "But Virgie gave it to you straight on Butman and the Widow. I had a hunch on that. You didn't do so damned much reforming, Ourney."

"I was after the big guys," I said. "You don't often get 'em, Donelly. You know that. They got Cherulli, right at the start. Maybe Cherulli was pretty big. Christenson wasn't so small. We got him out. And Virgie Beers was buying men to use as guns. We stopped her. Both of 'em were crime-breeders."

Donelly finished his gin, yawned.

"Yeah," he said slowly.

"How about the oval-faced kid?" I asked. "She helped Christenson try to frame me into telling something I didn't know. But maybe she never got a break. Got much on her?"

Donelly whistled softly. "Hell!" he said. His eyes narrowed on mine. "Her name's Louise Sarden. She's never been fingerprinted. You might come along to see

Lentz. You helped us a lot—we were pretty far behind you at times. You might sob a little for her.''

I nodded. "I might," I told him. "She might learn to be decent. I think she's got it in her. I sort of—like her.''

Donelly smiled. He didn't say anything. Phil Dobe poked one of the emerald cut pieces of green glass with a dirty finger.

"Cold stuff," he muttered.

"Goddam cold," Donelly said.

I stared down at the fused glass, shook my head slowly.

"Cold as—death," I said.

A man in the room next to mine was taking a bath and trying to make it easier by singing. Donelly scooped up the green stones and rose.

"If I had a voice like that I'd never *take* a bath," he muttered.

I told him he had a voice like that. Phil Dobe shoved back his chair and said he was heading toward his lousy sheet.

"There'll be something *in* it tomorrow," he said grimly.

I told them I was going to bed. By the time they had reached the door I had my vest off. After a while I called a number and asked for Louise Sarden. While I was waiting to hear her voice I smoked a cigarette and wondered why in hell I was calling her. It was probably a bad sign. I'd felt that way when I'd put up the bail money for her. But I'd put it up.

Her voice sounded tired.

I said: "This is Mal Ourney. I've been up later than this. Can I come over?''

She said that I could.

VINTAGE CRIME titles available from No Exit Press

Fast One – Paul Cain
0 948353 03 1 (hb) £9.95, 04 X (pb) £3.95

Possibly the toughest tough-guy story ever written. Set in Depression Los Angeles, it has a surreal quality that is positively hypnotic. It is the saga of gunman-gambler Gerry Kells and his dipsomaniacal lover S. Grandquist (she has no first name), who rearrange the Los Angeles underworld and 'disappear' in an explosive climax that matches their first appearance. The pace is incredible and the complex plot, with its twists and turns, defies summary.

The Dead Don't Care – Jonathan Latimer
0 948353 07 4 (hb) £9.95, 08 2 (pb) £3.95

Meet Bill Crane, the hardboiled P.I., and his two sidekicks O'Malley and Doc Williams. The locale of the cyclonic action is a large Florida estate near Miami. A varied cast includes a former tragic actress turned dipso, a gigolo, a 'Babe' from Minsky's, a broken-down welterweight and an exotic Mayan dancer. Kidnapping and murder give the final shake to the cocktail and provide an explosive and shocking climax.

Green Ice – Raoul Whitfield
0 948353 13 9 (hb) £9.95, 14 7 (pb) £3.95

Watch out for Mal Ourney: where Mal goes, murder follows. It is on his heels as he walks out of Sing Sing after taking a manslaughter rap for a dubious dame and follows him all the way on the trail of some sizzling hot emeralds – 'green ice'. 'Here are 280 pages of naked action, pounded into tough compactness by staccato, hammer-like writing.' – Dashiell Hammett.

Death in a Bowl – Raoul Whitfield
0 948353 23 6 (hb) £9.95, 24 4 (pb) £3.95

Maestro Hans Reiner is on the podium, taking the fiddle players through a big crescendo. Then something goes off with a bang and it is not the timpani. Reiner finds himself with a load of lead in the back – and a new tune: The Funeral March.

The Virgin Kills – Raoul Whitfield
0 948353 25 2 (hb) £9.95, 26 0 (pb) £3.95

More of the sharpest, toughest writing you will ever read – fast, lean, without an ounce of sentimentality. 'Raoul Whitfield holds up better than Ernest Hemingway.' – Pete Hamill.

If you want to obtain any of these titles, please send a cheque for the appropriate amount, plus 10% for p&p, to: **Oldcastle Books Ltd, 18 Coleswood Road, Harpenden, Herts AL5 1EQ.**